Rockett's World

WHERE DO YOU BELONG?

Read more about

Rockett's World
in:
#1 WHO CAN YOU
TRUST?
#2 WHAT KIND OF
FRIEND ARE YOU?
#3 ARE WE THERE
YET?
#4 CAN YOU KEEP A
SECRET?
#6 WHO'S
RUNNING THIS
SHOW?

Rockett's World

WHERE DO YOU BELONG?

Lauren Day

SCHOLASTIC INC.

New York Toronto London Auckland Sydney
Mexico City New Delhi Hong Kong

ISBN 0-439-08694-9

12 11 10 9 8 7 6 5 4 3 2 1   0 1 2 3 4 5/0

Printed in the U.S.A.   40
First Scholastic printing, March 2000

Rockett's World

WHERE DO YOU BELONG?

CHAPTER ONE

"Rockett! Hello. Hey. Earth to Rockett!"

In the busy hallway of Whistling Pines Junior High School, Jessie Marbella tried desperately to get her friend's attention.

"Rockett! Over here," she shouted, standing on tiptoe to wave over the heads of the noisy, jostling kids jamming the school corridor.

Rockett Movado was oblivious.

Head down, shoulders bent under the weight of her book-filled backpack, she plowed forward, unaware of her friend's plea. "Rockett! Help!" Jessie tried one last time and, finally, Rockett looked up.

"Oh, hi, Jessie," she responded absentmindedly.

"Can I talk to you for a sec?" her frantic bud called.

Trying to snap out of the whack mood that had ambushed her this morning, Rockett forced herself to smile. "Sure," she said, making her way to the wall of lockers where Jessie was waiting.

Through her blue funk, Rockett noted that her normally normal bud was wearing a coat. Why, she wondered, on such a mild Monday morning, was her friend dressed for a blizzard?

1

Her curiosity was quickly sidetracked by Jessie's question. "Are you okay, Rockett? You seemed kind of lost in space. Is something wrong?"

"Um . . . nothing major," Rockett answered with a shrug. "My sister, Juno, is coming home from college for a couple of days. And I just found out that she's going to be bunking with me."

Just found out is right.

Pass the milk, Rockett, and by the way, could you tidy up your room? Oh, and clear off the guest bed, okay? And maybe make a tiny bit of space in one of your drawers. You'll never guess who's going to be here tonight.

Gee, Mom, could it possibly be the most wonderful daughter a parent ever had — Juno Artemis Movado — who just happens to be named for goddesses?

She hadn't really said that aloud. She'd only thought it. Which made her feel bad enough.

No problem, Mom, she'd also imagined herself grumbling. *And while I'm at it, why don't I just take down all my posters and drawings, and sweep about a ton of choice material scraps under my bed? Hey, I don't need to make that patchwork bookbag I've spent weeks collecting fabric for! I mean, neatness counts and so, of course, does Juno.*

If she had actually let loose at breakfast this morning, her mom and dad and nine-year-old brother, Jasper, would've fully freaked. They'd have wondered if she'd gone mental on them.

Rockett wondered herself. How could anyone get bent out of shape over Juno?

2

But she had. She'd gotten so bummed that she hadn't even asked why Juno was coming home right in the middle of the semester. And, of course, nobody at the breakfast table had bothered to fill her in.

"Gee, that's great," Jessie was saying. "Someone to share your room with. It'll be like a pajama party. But, Rockett, I —"

"A pajama party?" Rockett said. "Not exactly. I mean, the truth is, my big sister's cool. She's majoring in computer graphics, fully acing her design courses. My parents are *so* proud of her."

"Computer graphics, that's nice," Jessie said politely. "But I was wondering —"

"Oh, yeah, Juno's practically perfect," Rockett babbled on. "Like, my dad offered to move all his stuff out of her room so she could have it back. He's taken it over since he's right in the middle of this major project that's due next week. And, of course, Juno was totally understanding. She just went, like, 'No biggie, Dad —'"

To tell the truth, her dad had also checked it out with her. He'd looked up from his cornflakes to say, "I hope it's okay with you. Is it, Rock? Because, otherwise, I'll clean out Juno's room today."

Hello. What was she supposed to say, "Break out the broom, Dad, 'cause no way am I sharing my sacred space with Saint Juno"?

"I wish I had a sister to hang with," Jessie said, "instead of just an older brother like Emilio, who's way too busy for me most of the time."

3

"Oh, that's right," Rockett finally remembered. "You were supposed to go fishing with Emilio yesterday. How'd it go?"

"Excellent." Jessie's blue eyes sparkled suddenly with excitement. "I mean, I had to beg him to take me along. And he made me promise not to be a pest. And I could not even look at, let alone squish, this gross little worm onto my hook. I used bread instead. And, of course, Emilio threw back everything he caught 'cause he's an animal lover like me and totally fish-friendly. But, Rockett, wait till you hear what happened —"

"Hey, Jessie," someone called, interrupting the revelation, "take off your coat and stay awhile."

The cheery voice belonged to cool and cocky Max Diamond, who had a little crush on Jessie. Predictably, the freckle-faced boy's remark was followed by a burst of appreciative laughter from his posse, The Ones.

Led by the Empress of Trendy, Nicole Whittaker, The Ones were Whistling Pines' most popular crew.

"I . . . um," Jessie stammered, hugging herself more tightly. "I can't!"

The Ones stopped and stared at her.

"Can't?" Nicole's manicured hands flew to her designer-clad hips. She cocked her blond head. "Excuse me?" she challenged.

Stephanie Hollis slipped her arm through Nicole's. "What are you hiding, Jessie?" she teased.

"Could she possibly be wearing some hand-me-

4

down outfit she got from her . . . *mummy?*" Nicole asked slyly.

The Ones blinked cluelessly at their leader.

"Mummy!" Nicole repeated impatiently, shaking off Stephanie's arm. "As in, bandaged dead person of Egyptian descent."

"That's Nicole's idea of funny," Jessie said. "'Cause my mom's an Egyptologist."

"Oh!" the other Ones exclaimed, finally getting the lame joke.

Whitney, Nicole's best friend and sidekick, quickly picked up on it. "Yeah, Jessie. Don't be so . . . *wrapped up* . . . in yourself. Get it?" She checked in with her buds. "Mummy. Wrapped up?"

"Duh." Stephanie rolled her eyes.

"She's wearing it to Mr. Baldus's home *tomb.* . . . Oops, I mean homeroom," Max's best bud, the tall, blond jockster Cleve, quipped.

"No way," Max chimed in. "Baldus is a zero, not a pharaoh."

There was a strange sound, a cross between a sneeze and a whimper. Jessie wriggled oddly, then clutched the collar of her coat.

The Ones were so busy high-fiving one another and chuckling at their puny puns that they apparently hadn't noticed the curious noise.

No one seemed to have heard it but Rockett — and Jessie, who shot her friend a pleading look, then sneezed loudly and, as far as Rockett was concerned, not very convincingly.

"I . . . I've got a cold," Jessie blurted out, turning her back on the in-crew.

"Ugh. That's all I need!" Nicole announced dramatically. "Time to move on, people. I've got way too much going on in my life at the moment to get sidelined by some random virus. I've got issues to deal with. Profound personal issues."

Stephanie and Whitney exchanged surprised looks.

"Really?" Stephanie quizzed Nicole. "Like what?"

"Tell!" Whitney prodded.

"Oh, like you chipped a nail?" Max teased.

Nicole shot him an icy look and he raised his hands in surrender.

"Nobody ever accused my man Max of being sensitive," Cleve pointed out, cracking up with his pal.

"Boys can be so hugely immature," Whitney noted, gazing supportively at Nicole.

"Meaning?" Max challenged.

"Can't you see that something's seriously stressing the girl?" Stephanie snapped. "Tell us, Nic. Share your pain."

"Hey, we were just kidding," Cleve apologized. "What's up for real, Nic?"

Nicole seemed about to speak. She hesitated, thought it over. Then she turned on her eager homeys.

"Stop salivating. It's so unattractive," she commanded. "Do I look like someone who'd unload a so-not-fixable problem on her best friends? I don't think so. Especially since I am the brightest member of this group!"

Wheeling away from her startled buds, she took off down the hall.

"A so-not-fixable problem?" Rockett mused aloud as The Ones scurried after their irate leader. "A dire personal dilemma? I wonder what's up?"

"I don't know," Jessie lamented, "but I know exactly how she feels — well, almost. I mean, I don't actually know *exactly* how Nicole feels, since I'm not fabulously fashionable," she amended, without a hint of sarcasm, "but in the dire dilemma department, we are so in sync today."

Rockett's heart went out to her friend. Maybe no one would ever call Jessie Marbella fabulously fashionable — especially judging by today's outfit — but she was one of the nicest, kindest, most generous people Rockett had ever met.

Hadn't Jessie been the first to befriend her, gone out of her way to make Rockett feel comfortable her first nerve-racking day at clique-conscious Whistling Pines? The girl was true blue, through and through.

So what had she meant, Rockett wondered, about being in sync with Nicole of all people?

"What's up, Jess?" she prodded.

"I was trying to tell you before The Ones invaded," Jessie replied. "It happened at the end of my fishing trip with Emilio. I need your help, Rockett."

Oh, no. Not today. Not with Juno showing up, Rockett couldn't help thinking. *I mean, I'm bummed that she's crashing in my room and that my parents are all, "Make way for the homecoming queen!" but, I've got to admit, I'm also kind of psyched.*

While my brilliant sister's racking up A's at college, I've been living in our new house, in our new town, making new friends in a new school. There's a lot Juno doesn't know about me and our life. I'm practically a new Rockett.

Of course, I want to help Jessie. She's my bud and I want to be there for her. But I've got too much on my mind right now. Her timing is way off.

"What kind of help, Jess?" Rockett asked carefully.

"Shhh, I . . ." Jessie cautioned. Then, with her back to the raucous flow of hall traffic, she opened her coat a smidge and motioned for Rockett to peek inside. "I mean," she added in a desperate whisper, "*we* need your help."

We?

Totally curious, Rockett peered inside her friend's coat.

Nestled in a peppermint-striped baby carrier strapped to Jessie's chest, a wriggling ball of dark fur huddled.

It made a noise, the same one Rockett had heard before — a whimper and then a little sneeze.

And then two big brown eyes shot open and stared brightly up at Rockett.

"What is it?" she gasped, stepping back, startled.

Brown and furry and beginning to stir now inside the cocoonlike carrier — what kind of creature was Jessie protecting so tenderly in her coat? Why had she brought whatever it was to school? And, Rockett wondered, exactly what kind of help did Jessie need?

Confession Session

I hate it when some-
one hints that something icky
is about to happen but they won't
tell you what. It's so Mavis, and way un-
Nic. Profound personal issues? Excuse me,
but what PPI could possibly be doggin'
Whistling Pines' golden girl? And why
won't she share it with me? Nicole is my
best friend, my main big, my true-blue
homey — but she can so get on my
one last nerve.

I'm glad Rockett's my friend. She's so creative. And I'm totally not. Look how I've messed up already — wearing a coat in practically a heat wave. Nice going, Jessie. But I had to hide the poor little guy. I couldn't leave him at home. And now if anyone at school finds out, we're in big trouble. I know Rockett won't let us down. She's our only hope.

I love a week that starts out weird. I mean, whew, what's the story on Jessie? I thought the babe was buff. Then she shows up wearing that whack outfit, acting all nervous. Something's rattling Nicole's cage, too. The girl's, like, in the middle of a meltdown. Man, it's only Monday. This week's shaping up to be fierce.

CHAPTER TWO

"It's a puppy," Jessie announced. "What did you think it was?"

"I don't know," Rockett murmured, staring in wide-eyed wonder at the tiny, precious creature. "A science project?"

Jessie giggled. "Isn't he adorable?"

Rockett had a wild urge to reach out and cuddle the squirming little dog. He was hardly more than a handful of shiny nose and brown curls.

Juno would have loved him, she caught herself thinking.

Well, of course. Juno loves puppies and cats and birds and fish and people and trees and computers, and she's just too totally perfect.

Then suddenly Jessie said, "We've just got to find him a home."

"Isn't he yours?" Rockett asked, startled.

"I wish. When Emilio and I were packing up yesterday, it started to pour. And this pathetic little soaking-wet puppy wandered out of the woods. There was no one else around. We were miles and miles from anywhere. I couldn't just leave him there all alone."

The little dog, which had been napping, was awake now, stretching and yawning. His big brown eyes were still fastened on Rockett.

"He is so cute. I can see why you and Emilio rescued him —" But what was he doing in school?

"Emilio didn't rescue him," Jessie blurted, blushing. "He doesn't know. He didn't see the puppy." She became very busy stroking the fur ball squirming against her T-shirt. Without looking up, she added, "He was so busy packing up his fishing gear he never even noticed. And all the way home he was practicing French, talking along with a language tape."

"So you smuggled him home?"

"I guess," Jessie allowed nervously.

"And what did your mom say?" Rockett asked with the sinking feeling that she already knew the answer.

Although she taught at the university, Jessie's mom, like Rockett's dad, did a lot of work at home. Jessie's house, Rockett knew, was filled with ancient art and precious Egyptian artifacts that Professor Marbella was studying and cataloging. She was not likely to welcome a soaking-wet stray puppy, however adorable, to romp through her priceless collection.

"Um . . . she doesn't know, either," Jess confessed, confirming Rockett's suspicion. "I hid him in my room last night. He totally mangled one of my old denim sneakers. My mom would never let me keep him with all her valuable stuff around the house. And I can't have him at my dad's place, either."

Rockett shook her head thoughtfully. "Sounds like trouble, Jessie."

Jessie brightened. "Trouble. That's what we'll call him. That's a great name, Rockett — just for now."

"But you can't keep him —" Rockett began.

"I know, I know, I know," her friend cut her off. "But I couldn't just leave him in the woods, could I? He was all shivering and helpless and alone."

"I guess not," Rockett conceded, "but then what are you going to do? What's the plan?"

"Track down his true owner, I guess, or else find him a wonderful new home."

"Sounds good," Rockett said, aware by the way kids were speeding by them that, any minute now, the homeroom bell would sound and they'd be late to class.

"Well, that's where you come in," Jessie said. "We'll have to get started right after school."

After school? I can't, Rockett thought. *I've gotta finish getting my room ready for La Juno. I'll do what I can, but what's this* we *business?*

But there were even more urgent issues.

"Okay, Jessie. Reality check. What are you going to do with him today? Like right now? You can't wear your coat in class without everyone wanting to know why."

"I know," Jessie admitted forlornly. "I was thinking of taking him to Principal Herrera's office and leaving him there until after lunch. But then I thought, she'll call my mom. Or worse, send him to the pound!"

"Not even. She'd never," Rockett said, alarmed. Trouble, she was starting to think, was certainly the right name for the puppy.

14

"We've got to find someone who can take care of him. Just until we can get him a good home," Jessie was saying. "That's why I need your help. You're the best, Rockett. You're so creative. You always come up with great ideas. You've got to help me. Please."

Creative? If I were really creative I'd come up with a quick way to say no to Jessie without trashing our friendship. What was she thinking, bringing a dog to school? Okay, the little guy is adorable and in dire need of rescuing. And I'm so flattered that Jessie thinks I can help. But I've got my own priorities. Cramming a ton of stuff under my bed and finding a hiding place for my journal may not seem important, but I so don't want a lecture on how Generous Juno does everything right and I can't even clear a dresser drawer for her.

Jessie should have thought things through before she plopped the puppy into that baby carrier.

I mean, I could probably come up with a gazillion ideas for tracking down the pup's rightful owner. Eventually. But the immediate problem — finding a safe space to stash him — is more . . . well, immediate. I should help — just for now.

Okay, compromise. Jessie's your bud. Think, Rockett, think! You can help her find a way to hide the puppy — just for now.

"We don't have much time, Jess," Rockett found herself saying. "Like maybe you could stash him in your locker till after homeroom."

But even as Jessie's face brightened, Rockett saw the drawback to that scheme. "And what, gag him so he doesn't bark, whimper, or sneeze? Duh, excellent notion.

15

Not," she decided. "I wish my backpack were big enough . . ."

"And just happened to contain food, water, and a decent supply of oxygen," Jessie said sadly. "Nope. I thought of that. It won't work. Unless someone has a backpack with mesh sides like one of those pet carriers."

"Like someone would just happen to show up at school today lugging an empty pet carrier. Dream on," Rockett advised.

"And while we're at it," Jessie said, glancing nervously at the hall clock, "we'd better start dreaming up an excuse for why we're going to be late for homeroom."

"Omigosh, Jessie, look! I must be seeing things," Rockett exclaimed, staring openmouthed at the trio of girls hurrying down the hall toward them.

"Uh, no," Jessie said. "It's just the CSGs."

Astrologically bonded, the CSGs — or Cool Sagittarius Girls — Nakili, Miko, and Dana, were best buds whose birthdays all fell in November or December under the sign of Sagittarius.

Rockett had hit it off with Miko and Nakili, but Dana St. Clair had so made it clear that she was not a fan.

Luckily, it wasn't Dana toting the object that excited Rockett's attention.

"Jessie, do you see what I see? What's Nakili carrying?"

Jessie squinted in Nakili's direction. "Looks like a rug with handles," she said.

"And mesh panels at the ends?"

"Well, yeah. It does look like that. Like a gym bag

16

made of one of those cool native fabrics Nakili loves. I know you're into original-looking stuff, Rockett, interesting fabrics and materials and all. But the bell's going to ring any minute —"

"Or a very fancy dog carrier?"

Jessie was trying to calm the rowdy little puppy wriggling happily under her coat. She looked up, blinking at Rockett. "A what?"

"Jessie, it's the best I can come up with at the moment. We've got to convince Nakili to let us use that bag."

"Would she have to know about Trouble?" Jessie asked, panicked.

"Well, yes. We can't just slip him into her gym bag or whatever it is without her knowing about it."

"I'm not sure," Jessie said tensely as the pup squirmed in his carrier. "I wasn't thinking about letting anyone else know that I brought the puppy to school. I thought it would just be you and me. That we'd work it out."

"I think we can work it out," Rockett assured her as the CSGs spotted them and Miko began to wave. "And it totally hinges on Nakili's generosity."

And Dana's mood, Rockett thought. *Just our luck. The best bag for the job is walking alongside one of the biggest mouths. Jessie's worrying about Nakili knowing. I'm wondering if Dana would blow our cover. What if she decided to report us to Mrs. Herrera? But would she? Can we take the chance? There must be some way we can keep Dana from finding out about Trouble — and still get Nakili to help.*

CHAPTER THREE

"What's the matter with you?" Dana St. Clair stared at Jessie as if she were studying an insect under a microscope. "Why are you wiggling like that? Are you supposed to be doing some kind of dance?"

"I'm . . . I'm not dancing," Jessie said, buttoning the collar of her coat.

"And what's with the outerwear?" Dana persisted.

"Nakili." Rockett stepped between Dana and Jessie. "Where did you get that awesome bag?"

Nakili Abuto grinned gratefully. Her beaded earrings and multiple bracelets rattled as she turned, modeling the beautiful bag for Rockett.

"Hey, Rockett. Hi, Jessie." Miko Kajiyama beamed at them through her pointy-tipped, black-rimmed glasses. "Isn't it excellent? Nakili's dad had it made for her in Morocco."

"On his last buying trip," Nakili added, reminding Rockett that her friend's father, Farouto, was an Oriental rug dealer. "It's a kilim."

"That's a kind of rug," Miko explained. "Aren't the colors cool? It's for carrying her Rollerblades."

"He even had the mesh sides put in so my skates

would stay fresh and I could stow extra socks and gear," Nakili said.

"It's amazing, totally beautiful," Rockett said honestly.

"Too beautiful," Jessie blurted out. "I mean, it could get . . . um, damaged."

Everyone stared at her. "Like how?" Miko asked.

"I mean, like if something inside it got, well, wet. I don't know. Like, um, sweaty socks?"

"Wet?" Rockett asked Jessie.

"Yes, you know," Jessie whispered. "What if you-know-who has, like, an accident?"

"Sweaty socks is way more than I want to know about that bag," Dana said.

"No problem. The inside is totally waterproof," Nakili told Jessie. "My dad had it lined like a gym bag so my rank socks and stuff wouldn't ruin it."

"That's perfect!" Jessie said, psyched.

"Your dad's brilliant," Rockett agreed enthusiastically. "So are your Rollerblades in there?"

"Not yet. Just my soccer uniform and some extra T-shirts and socks and stuff."

"But, ah, excuse me?" Dana said. "Did I miss the answer to my question or should I make it multiple choice? What," she asked Jessie, "are you doing in an overcoat and why were you squirming? Is it, A, to disguise the fact that you had a monster growth spurt this morning and now your clothes are so tight they're giving you under-arm wedgies? B, because you caught a gross itchy disease that needs to be kept warm? Or C, and I'm guessing it's this one, you've got something to hide?"

Jessie gazed pleadingly at Rockett.

"She's got a cold," Rockett improvised.

"Yeah, right," Dana grumbled. "Excuse me? Nothing personal, Nakili. I mean, I think your Rollerblade bag's the bomb, but something is way ripe here."

Suddenly inspired, Rockett remembered. "How's Marlo, Dana?" she asked.

"Marlo, my golden retriever?" Dana was flustered.

"And Yuppy and Bubby?" Rockett said.

"She means Ippy and Bippy," Nakili explained to Dana.

Dana's face softened lovingly. "My itty-bitty little fishies?" she asked, then added suspiciously, "Why do you want to know?"

"Dana gets furiously mushy over pets," Nakili said.

"You like animals?" Jessie asked, surprised.

"I do," Dana responded.

"Me too," said Miko.

"Well, who doesn't?" Dana huffed. "I mean, it's, like, so cold not to."

"Let's do it," Rockett decided. "It's now or never, Jess. We've got exactly ten seconds to make it to homeroom before the bell."

Jessie nodded, gulped, then opened her coat. "His name's Trouble," she whispered.

The CSGs gathered around, stared, and gasped.

"Look. A puppy. Ooooh, it's so cute," Miko crooned.

"I love puppies," Nakili squealed. "Wow, Jessie, where did you get it?"

Dana shouldered her best buds aside and reached for the happy little dog. "Oh, d'poor bootiful bay-bee," she purred, lifting the puppy out of the striped baby carrier.

Rockett grinned at Jessie, who was staring at Dana with her mouth flopped open.

"I warned you." Nakili giggled.

"Nakili, can we keep him in your bag, just until first period?" Rockett asked. "Just till we can find someone else to take care of him? Jessie found him in the woods. He's homeless. I'll explain on the way to class."

"Do it, Nakili," Dana urged. "Look at the 'ittle cootie pie. Look at the doggie-poggie. Mama's gonna give 'im a ride in Nakili's bootiful bag."

"Well, okay." Nakili caved in with a grin. "But just until first period, right?"

Whew! Glad I remembered how much Dana loves her dog, Marlo, Rockett thought as they tucked the pup into a nest of laundry-fresh tees and sweats inside Nakili's bag. *And how cool is it that Nakili's skate carrier has vents and is waterproof? We definitely did the right thing letting the CSGs in on our secret. Not everyone's going to be up for helping Jessie. Anyone could decide to blow the whistle on us. We got lucky with Dana. But no one else needs to know.*

I mean, if I wind up in Mrs. Herrera's office over this puppy, my parents will freak. They'll remind me how Juno would never have risked detention. Juno never messes up.

Whoops, there goes the bell — and here comes Trouble!

21

Confession Session

Dana's been down on Rockett since day one. I can't believe she's done this major turnaround. Or that Rockett trusted her with such a serious secret. I just hope neither of them rocks the boat, 'cause if anyone else finds out that there's a puppy in homeroom, Nakili and Jessie are going to be toast.

My father's gonna flip if Trouble messes up my Rollerblade bag. I didn't have time to think about that with Dana going mental over the puppy. If I tell my dad how pressured I felt, he won't buy it. I know what he'll say: If Dana told you to jump off the roof, does that mean you have to do it? Ugh. What do fathers know about best-bud bonding?

CHAPTER FOUR

"Good morning, my tardies," Mr. Baldus called out as Rockett, Jessie, and the CSGs burst breathlessly into homeroom.

Everyone turned to stare, of course. Which was exactly what they didn't need. Especially since Dana was acting so flipped.

She had decided to protect the puppy by "hiding" Nakili.

Dana buzzed awkwardly around her bud, trying to shield her from curious eyes. In her black skirt and tights and a bright yellow shirt she looked like a bumblebee, Rockett thought.

Instead of carrying the bag with the puppy in it over her shoulder, Nakili was cradling it in her bracelet-jangling arms.

Nearly panting aloud, Miko hurried behind them, so loaded down with their books she was practically bow-legged.

"Think anyone will notice?" Jessie asked Rockett as they scooted to their desks.

Rockett glanced around. The entire class had swiveled in their seats to watch the CSGs' weird entrance. Only their ponytailed homeroom teacher seemed unaware of the parade.

Suddenly Rockett wondered if it had been smart to tell the CSGs about Trouble. She'd thought Dana would keep the secret — but she hadn't counted on Dana not being able to leave the dog alone!

"Glad you could join us for the most happenin' class of the day," Mr. Baldus was saying, rifling through a mess of papers on his desk. "Homeroom. It's as vital as OJ for kickin' off the A.M. —"

"Mr. Baldus doesn't have a clue," Rockett tried to re-assure Jessie.

Nakili slipped into the seat behind Rockett, still clutching the Rollerblade bag to her heart.

"Attention, people. Eyes front and center." Mr. Baldus looked up just as Nakili's satchel stirred in her arms.

Nearby, Rockett saw Sharla squinting suspiciously at the bag.

Oh, no, she thought. If anyone could spell trouble for Trouble, it was Sharla Rae Norvell. She was all attitude. The only thing Sharla seemed to like about animals was how they looked on her — like that stretchy leopard print skirt she was wearing, Rockett noted, and the zebra-striped handkerchief around her neck.

"Let us check out the happenings that will make history at Whistling Pines this week. What's this?" Mr. Baldus tilted his head to study the paper he'd pulled from the pile on his desk.

There was a muffled sneeze and a whimper.

Sharla's dark eyes widened.

"I seem to have snagged a cafeteria menu. Let's see, now. If it's Monday, it must be meat loaf," Mr. Baldus announced.

The puppy's whimpering was buried beneath a barrage of boos and hisses.

Sharla looked up suddenly. Her eyes locked on Rockett's.

Heart pounding, Rockett smiled at the now-grinning rebel girl.

"Meat loaf? You mean hurl loaf," Max called out.

Unaware of Sharla's interest, Jessie tugged at Rockett's sleeve. "Meat loaf's perfect!" she exclaimed, then lowered her voice. "For you-know-who," she added in a whisper.

"What, did you resign from the VWA — Vegetarian Wimps of America?" Sharla cackled.

Alarmed at having been overheard, Jessie gazed tensely at Rockett and began nibbling on her nails.

"Mr. Baldus, yo, Mr. B," Ruben hollered, waving his arm, the sleeve of his zippered sweatshirt flapping. "If I guess what Mr. Pill's meat loaf is made of, do I win the contest?"

"What's the prize?" Cleve yelled gleefully across the room to Ruben.

"You get to eat lunch at another school," Max answered.

Mavis Wartella-Depew looked up from the magazine horoscope she'd been studying. "Is there a contest?" she asked, absently blinking through her thick, square glasses.

"Class, come to order," Mr. Baldus demanded. Then with a cagey smile he added, "And I don't mean come to order . . . *meat loaf*."

"Speaking of lunch meat." Stephanie studied Mavis's brown outfit. "What thrift shop did you snag that dress at?"

"Eeeuww. It looks like meat loaf with buttons." Whitney cringed.

Both girls turned expectantly to Nicole, who rolled her eyes and sighed heavily. "Boring," she murmured dully. "Next."

Unconcerned, Mavis stuffed the 'zine she'd been browsing into the oversized shoulder bag at her feet.

Rockett saw the tip of Mavis's Ouija board sticking out of the burlap bag, and a videocassette that was probably one of the old horror movies Mavis loved. Who knew what else was stowed in that bottomless pit of portable weirdness? Astrology charts, maybe, incense sticks, stones alleged to have magical powers. It could be any of the bizarre gear that Mavis dragged with her daily.

Mavis shrugged. She warned, "Scoff if you wish to risk the wrath of the universe by unbelieving, but certain thinking-highly-of-themselves personages are likely to fly for a bad fall. Even today."

Nicole looked up. "What did you say?" she snapped. "What do you mean by that?"

"What goes up must come down," Mavis answered mysteriously.

"Watch out, Nicole, she's psychic," Arnold Zeitbaum said sarcastically.

"You mean psycho," Sharla sneered.

Dana snickered, then noticed Sharla staring at Nakili's backpack. "Don't you hate meat loaf?" she asked quickly, trying to divert Sharla's attention.

"Naw, I love it," Sharla stubbornly insisted. "Pill's meat loaf is the best, the bomb, positively phat. The middle is so raw you can scoop it out and stuff it into some unsuspecting sap's soccer shoes."

"That is so ill," Nakili blurted out.

Sharla Rae Norvell glared dangerously at her.

"She means, it'll get you ill," Rockett said quickly.

Mr. Baldus continued shuffling through his mail, chuckling and mumbling to himself, then sharing selected announcements with the class. "Oh, here's a good one," he decided. "Cell phones are prohibited on the baseball fields. Guess the pitcher and catcher will have to go back to hand signals."

"I'll hold the bag," Dana hissed to Nakili, leaping to her feet, "to protect . . . you know, your skates or whatever. I'm not saying you aren't doing an excellent job, only you don't have a . . . Well, you know. You don't have *experience*."

Rockett glanced over at Jessie, who was watching Dana and speed-chomping her nails now. Her heart sank at the sight of her stressed-out bud.

27

How can a good deed go so brutally bad? Jessie didn't want me to tell anyone. But we needed help, so I convinced her we could confide in the CSGs. I just didn't count on Dana going postal over the puppy. She is so going to blow our cover.

Sharla had been watching Dana, too. "What's with the bag?" she demanded.

"Nothing!" Jessie assured her.

"Nakili's dad had it made for her in Africa," Miko started to explain. "Isn't it excellent? It's made of an indigenous Moroccan rug fabric woven into a classic native design known as kilim."

"Whoa, encyclopedia-girl," Sharla commanded.

She looked from Miko to Dana to Nakili to Jessie, who was furiously gnawing on her pinky nail. Her dark eyes finally rested on Rockett.

Uh-oh, she's going to ask me, point-blank, straight ahead, to tell her what's in the bag. This is all Dana's fault! What am I going to do?

"Yo, Nicole!" Ruben shouted, laughing. "Pill's meat loaf is seriously lethal. You're the student body president. What are you going to do about it?"

The class grew quiet. All heads turned toward Nicole.

She seemed for a moment so lost in thought that she was unaware of everyone's attention.

Whitney loudly cleared her throat. Finally, Nicole looked up. "What?" she growled.

"Um, Ruben was talking to you," Stephanie said cautiously.

"He wants to know what you're going to do about Mr. Pill's meat loaf," Max said.

Like an awakened shark, Nicole snapped out of her funk. "What would you do, Max?" she hissed. "Like, do it! I've got more pressing matters to concern myself with than a couple of cases of food poisoning in the school barfeteria."

"I seem to have gotten Mrs. Herrera's mail this morning," Mr. Baldus mused aloud. "Someone must've slipped it into my mailbox by mistake. Oops, here's her schedule. Teacher conferences this morning. Lunch with the district superintendent. And, what's this? Nicole, your parents are coming to see our esteemed principal this afternoon."

"No!" Nicole gasped before realizing that all eyes were on her again. "I mean, *know* that."

With a flip of her wrist, she tossed back her head. "As if Reginald and Celeste don't share everything with me. Like, duh. They're my parents."

She scrambled to her feet. "May I be excused?" she asked.

Before Mr. Baldus could respond, Nicole grabbed the hall pass and ran out of the room.

"Wassup with her?" Ruben wanted to know.

Max shrugged and looked at Cleve.

"Don't ask me," Cleve said as Mr. Baldus began to take attendance.

"Nakili Abuto," he called, then asked, "Dana, is there some reason you're standing in the aisle?"

29

"No," Dana answered meekly. "I mean, yes. I mean, I just wanted to get something from Nakili."

"Yeah, right." Sharla snorted.

Dana glared at her as Mr. Baldus moved on, then turned back to Nakili. "Can I hold . . . you know, can I hold . . . the bag?"

"Not now," Nakili whispered.

Rockett looked over at Sharla. Her brow was furrowed as she studied the two CSGs.

"Excuse me?" Dana said, all huffy. "Why not?"

"Because I think it's asleep," Nakili answered.

"It's asleep?" Suddenly Sharla's brow smoothed, her little brown eyes lit up, and her mouth twisted into a grin.

"Oh, is that another fabulous thing Moroccan rugs are famous for?" she challenged sarcastically. "They wiggle. They make little lame noises. And they *snooze*. You guys are pitiful," Sharla declared.

Mr. Baldus shouted, "Rockett Movado. Rockett. Are you with us today?"

"I guess," Rockett called back. She could feel herself blushing even as she tried hard to smile.

Ruben's easy laughter helped her. Rockett grinned at him gratefully, but her mind was racing.

I should have known Dana was going to mess things up. She thinks she's the only one who knows anything about dogs. And she's so bossy. If she doesn't get her way, there's no telling what she might do. Easy, girl, Rockett reminded herself, *you can't be sure Sharla knows what's in the bag.*

The bell rang, startling Rockett. She gathered up her things and hurried to help Miko with the CSGs' books.

Nakili was startled, too. She jumped at the sound of the bell. And suddenly the beautiful bag she'd hugged all period was alive and hopping.

"Careful," Dana commanded, rushing Nakili toward the door.

Rockett saw Sharla tearing after them.

Maybe I should tell her, she suddenly thought. *I mean, she's already suspicious. Everyone treats Sharla like such an outsider. I bet she'd be glad to be on the inside for a change. Plus, it would be way better to have her with us than against us. It can't hurt to have one more person know, can it?*

She had just about convinced herself to let Sharla in on the secret when she saw the rebel bump into Nakili accidentally-on-purpose.

"Yo, what's up with that skate bag, blade-girl?" Rockett heard Sharla sneer. "Could it possibly have . . . fleas?"

Confession Session

I had to get out of home-room. Between that deranged prophet of doom, Mavis, ranting that The Ones are heading for a fall, and Baldus breaking the news that Reginald and Celeste are visiting the principal today, I was about to die. Everyone thinks that my life is a bowl of cherries. It was, until I discovered the heinous secret my selfish parents have been harboring. Now it's just the pits.

Dana is a terminal dork. Like I really care what fugitive critter is hiding in Nakili's bag. Not! But, hmmm, wassup with her Oneness, Nicole the Nasty? She's way more tightly wrapped than usual. Don't tell me that the pushy princess is experiencing distress. Now there's a mystery I'd really like to unravel.

CHAPTER FIVE

"How is he? How is he? How is he?" Dana chanted the minute they were outside Mr. Baldus's room. "Let me see. Is he okay?"

"Ugh, chill out," Sharla groaned.

Then, muscling between Dana and Nakili, she peered into the bag.

"No, don't," Jessie gasped.

But Rockett saw Sharla's face. Just for a moment, the tough mask lifted. The permanent sneer was replaced with a look of awe and wonder.

"It's not what you think, Sharla," Jessie cautioned.

Sharla Rae's mask fell back into place.

"Oh, you mean there's not some sniveling little pooch in Nakili's oh-so-authentic African pouch?" she chided. "As if I cared."

"Uh, Rockett, I've gotta go," Nakili said nervously as Dana began cooing again to the puppy inside the bag. "I can't be late for English today. And I can't take Trouble with me. We have to take a quiz."

Miko added, "And it's going to majorly count toward our final grade."

Dana straightened up abruptly. "Tiny-doll's quiz. Omigosh, I totally forgot. Take good care of my 'ittle puppy-poo," she said, hurrying away.

Whew, Rockett thought as Dana disappeared into the crowd changing classes, *that's a relief. Dana's done everything but put an ad in the school paper that we're trying to hide a dog.* But her comfort didn't last long.

"No kidding, you guys. I've gotta go." Nakili gently lifted Trouble out of her skate bag. "Who's gonna hold him this period?"

"With friends like you, the pooch doesn't need enemies." Sharla sighed impatiently and thrust out her arms. "Right here, Nakili," she grumbled. "If you're gonna dump him, can the apologies and just take off."

"That's not fair," Nakili said, handing Sharla the puppy. "I'm really, really sorry. Honest," she told Rockett and Jessie. "See you guys at lunch, okay? We'll figure something out," she promised, then hurried away.

"But who's going to watch him now?" Jessie asked frantically. "I still need someone to help keep him safe for a whole period."

Rockett looked at Sharla.

Okay, so if you checked out warm and loving in the dictionary, you might not find Sharla Rae Norvell's picture. But look at her with Trouble. She sounds like she couldn't care less, yet unlike some people who baby-talk and bolt, she's reliable, nonflaky, and totally stand-up. Plus, who could better protect the pup from prying eyes? No one would dare challenge Sharla.

I think she's like a s'more — sticky and hard on the out-

side, *but marshmallow fluff inside. Juno showed me how to make them.*

Rockett said exactly what she was thinking. "Looks like Trouble here likes you."

Sharla froze. "No way," the bad blond warned. "Don't even think about it. I'm just holding him for a minute. That's all."

"Then I guess it's up to me," Jessie said, "even if everyone gets suspicious about the way I'm dressed." In desperation, she began strapping on the baby carrier and struggling into her coat again. "I'll take him to social studies with me. I mean, what else can we do?"

Hopelessly, Rockett looked around, searching for a hiding place for the puppy. She patted her own skirt pockets. They were way too small to even consider. And her backpack had no air vents.

"Ask Mavis," Sharla suggested sarcastically as the rumpled fortune-teller approached, the strap of her burlap shoulder bag mashing the front of her wrinkled vest.

"Mavis?" Rockett mused.

"Sure." Sharla laughed. "She's the one who sees the future. She thinks she's prophetic, but she's just pathetic. Maybe she'll tell you what will happen to your dog."

Mavis! We're in the same class next period. I bet she'd do it — take care of Trouble at least through science lab. She's definitely capable of keeping a secret. But what about the flake factor? Of course, this is one time when her rep for weirdness might work in our favor. I mean, she could wrap the puppy around her neck and call it a magical dog scarf, and everyone would just go, "Typical Mavis." Plus — boing! — there's her burlap bag. Emptied of 'zines and books and Ouija boards and sacred rocks, it would make a perfect puppy dog nest. It's just like the bag our neighbor Mrs. Potts carries her little poodle around in.

But will Mavis do it? For someone who's always making predictions, she's way unpredictable. Mavis likes to be helpful, but she can be stubborn and bossy, too.

And then there's Arnold . . .

In a short-sleeved green shirt buttoned all the way up to his Adam's apple, Arnold Zeitbaum was heading their way, too, lost in thought.

Seeing them coming, Jessie quickly reached for Trouble, who was wriggling in Sharla's hands and chewing on a corner of her zebra-striped handkerchief.

Sharla handed over the puppy reluctantly, it seemed to Rockett.

Happily panting and squirming, Trouble leaped into Jessie's arms. The little dog gave a yip of delight as she tucked him back into the warmth of her coat.

None of the crowd streaming by seemed to have noticed. Not even Arnold or Mavis had heard the noise.

Rockett studied the mismatched pair. *Sharla won't help us. Dana's a mess. And Miko and Nakili can't do it right now. I know Jessie wants to keep Trouble under wraps, but we need more help. Mavis may be our best shot. . . .*

"I sense a serious rift in the cosmos by the vibrations

of the stressful secret-like stuff here," the short soothsayer greeted them.

"I'd guess that happens a lot when you show up." Sharla cackled. "Hey, Zitbomb, how's life in the slow lane? Or is it overly optimistic to assume you've got a life?"

Pushing his sliding glasses back up the bridge of his nose, Arnold ignored her. "Greetings, fair princess," he said to Rockett. "You seem deep in thought. Anything I can do to improve your disposition?"

"I'm going to improve mine," Sharla said, "by splitting. Good luck with your problem, Rockett. I'm sure the interplanetary EMS squad will be tons of help."

"A problem?" Arnold said as Sharla left. "Did she say you have a problem?" he asked Rockett. Behind his thick, smudged lenses, his eyes looked moist with concern. "Oh, tell me, my lady, that I can be of service to you."

"Don't deal with this wrinkled brain-clod, Rockett! You should know by now that any help Zit-Wit offers is sure to end in ultimate disaster." Mavis turned and hissed at Arnold. "Go away, delusional alien detective! The problem here requires feminine intuitive skills beyond yourself."

"Aroint thee, halitosis harridan!" snapped Arnold. "My deductive brain is more than a match for your mumbo-jumbo jitters!"

"Why don't you go and console her queenly Oneness,

Moron of Zoron? I just saw her down the hall and she was totally vibrating weepy badness. Yuck."

"I don't know about Nicole," Jessie jumped in, "but you're right about us."

"That's 'cause we need help," Rockett pointedly reminded Jessie. "From everyone or anyone. A problem shared is a problem halved, my sister, Juno, says."

"Halved?" Jessie said miserably. "This one's in more like a billion pieces."

She was right, Rockett thought. Thanks to her hot hunch, they'd let the CSGs in on the puppy problem. Then Dana went into bonehead mode and put Sharla in the picture. Then Sharla suggested Mavis. It was almost hard to call Jessie's secret a secret anymore.

"But we don't have much choice, do we?" Jessie admitted nervously, and when Rockett said, "Not really," she took a deep breath and quickly filled Mavis and Arnold in on the puppy predicament. "So, until we can locate his owner or find him a good new home," Jessie finished up hopefully, "we were wondering — ?"

"Wondering . . . what?" Mavis put her fingers to her forehead, like a mind reader. "Ah, I'm getting it. The message is coming in now. . . ."

Jessie and Rockett exchanged questioning glances, but Arnold burst out impatiently, "Did you scuff your crystal ball bowling, mental midget? They want you to watch Trouble next period, of course."

"I know," Mavis said crossly. "I was being quite amusing. As I would have announced if you were not so

38

quickly blabbing, medieval mind-blot! And I would be glad to help out, but I've got science lab with Mr. Shuliss, Rockett. How am I going to hide a puppy in there?"

"Wait, wait." Now Arnold put his fingers to his forehead. "I'm getting a picture here. It's a . . . a . . . a big, empty burlap shoulder bag."

"Omigosh," Jessie gasped, "that would be so perfect. How did you think of it, Arnold?"

"The good Lady Rockett was staring at it the entire time she told her sad tale," he explained. "Mavis's poor purse is a solution, but sadly temporary. We need to be thinking permanent placement here. Finding his owner."

"We?" Rockett perked up at the word. "Then you're in, Arnold?" she asked excitedly. "You're going to help us, too?"

"Naturally," the brainiac announced.

"Welcome *a-board*," Mavis quipped, holding the Ouija board she'd removed from her purse. "Jessie, can you help me make room for the puppy? I would not leave this task to the disaster-prone bungler of the species."

"Jess, can I borrow your coat and the carrier?" Rockett asked. "While you guys get Mavis's bag ready for Trouble, I'll go get him some water."

"Water. Of course," Jessie said. "I figured meat loaf for lunch, but I forgot he'd need water. Poor sleepy little guy, he must be thirsty."

While Mavis rummaged through her bag, Jessie helped Rockett into her coat and gently transferred the baby carrier in which Trouble was drowsing contentedly.

"Arnold," Rockett said as his arms were filling with everything from books to a sequined turban, "we're going to meet the CSGs in the cafeteria at lunchtime to come up with a plan."

"I'll be there," Arnold said.

"Doubt me if you dare, Zeit-clod," Mavis said, "but the puppy's not the entire all that's troubling Rockett. Or Nicole. My tingle tells the truth. It's something," she declared menacingly, "way closer to home."

Even wrapped in Jessie's bulky coat, with the warm little puppy snuggled against her, Rockett felt a sudden chill.

"I'll meet you in front of science lab as soon as I can," she promised Mavis, hurrying away.

She had to get back before the bell rang, she told herself as she flew down the hall, brushing past kids coming the other way. But she suspected that it was Mavis's words and not the bell she was trying to outrun.

Home? Is Mavis picking up Juno's visit? Could that really be what she meant? Yuck, it would be so embarrassing to have Mavis, or anyone, know how I feel about my very own sister. I love Juno. She's the greatest. Who wouldn't love her? She's so smart. And helpful. And beautiful in her special Juno way. Not like a movie star or a model, but there's a goodness in her that kind of glows out. That's part of the problem. My big sister's too lovable. She's got all the answers and all the talent and, on top of it all, she's nice. How can I feel so bad about someone so good? It doesn't make any sense.

Maybe, Rockett thought as she rushed down the hall,

if I hadn't gotten all wrapped up in Jessie's problem, I'd have time to figure out what's up with me and my sister. This is so not what I planned.

How am I ever gonna get my room cleaned and my head clear for Juno's visit now that I've got this ball of Trouble rolling . . . ?

Confession Session

Emilio says, "Be careful what you wish for." Like if you wish for rain, you might wind up needing a rowboat. Well, pass the oars, 'cause I asked *one* person for help and now half the class knows there's a puppy on the premises.

CHAPTER SIX

One minute she was racing along the crowded corridor. The next, she was reeling backward. Two arms reached out to steady her. "Whoa, new girl."

She had run into someone. She felt the puppy stir sleepily against her. Hugging her coat, she looked up — into Ruben's grinning face. "What's the haps? Where you rushing?"

"To the gym," she answered. The girls' room would be too busy during class changeover, she'd decided. But she could get water for the pup at the sports center. Even if kids were changing in the locker room, the shower stalls were usually empty until the end of the period.

"What's your hurry? You on a mission?" Ruben asked.

Rockett laughed. "Sort of. A mission of mercy, I guess."

"Sounds like trouble," Ruben said.

Rockett was shocked. "How did you know?"

He scratched his head, mussing his thick black hair. "I think I missed a beat here. What am I supposed to know?"

"About Trouble," Rockett said.

"Well, that isn't very flattering." Ruben frowned and clutched his heart, acting hurt.

"No, I don't mean that kind of trouble," she explained without thinking. "I mean, Trouble, the puppy."

"Sorry, you'll have to speak slower or explain faster. I am seriously not getting this conversation," Ruben said. Then he grinned again, bigger and wider than ever. "Unless, of course, you mean *el perro loco*, the wild little dog that was hiding out in Nakili's new skate bag."

"You noticed it in homeroom, right?"

"Well, I had my suspicions," he said. "Then Dana clued me in two minutes ago. She didn't mean to, I don't think. She was just asking everyone whether they'd lost a puppy up near the lake this weekend."

Asking everyone? Oh, no, Rockett thought miserably. *This is all my fault. If I hadn't insisted on telling that motor-mouth, Jessie's secret wouldn't be all over the school.*

But I'm not sorry Ruben knows.

"Will you help us?" she asked softly, not wanting to wake the sleeping pup. "A bunch of people are going to meet at lunch to try to figure out how to find his owner."

"Hey, any dog named Trouble is a friend of mine," Ruben teased. "Catch you later."

Rockett watched him disappear into the crowd. *Ruben's a great guy to have on our side. And, yes, okay, I'm kinda crushed on him besides. But if Dana keeps blabbing, the wrong people are going to find out.*

"Rockett! Rockett Movado. I want to see you right now."

She looked up to see Mr. Shuliss racing toward her. The mild-mannered science teacher seemed to have something urgent on his mind.

Rockett gulped. When Ruben said Dana was asking *everyone*, could that have meant teachers, too?

"Um, hi, Mr. Shuliss," she mumbled, hugging the coat closed and tightening her grip on the warm lump of puppy snoozing inside. "You, um, want to see me?"

"There's something I want to know," the science-meister confirmed. He stared piercingly at her through his half-moon glasses. "Do you think Einstein was right when he said, 'Imagination is more important than knowledge'?"

Struck dumb, she gaped at him.

"I thought it might be a perfect slogan for our school paper. It might give students the inspiration they need! What do you think? You work on the paper, don't you?"

Rockett nodded. "It's, um, interesting," she managed to croak.

"Good. Well," he said, "you're coming to class, aren't you?"

"Definitely. Totally. I've just got . . . a quick errand to run," she babbled.

"See you in lab, then. 'Imagination is more important than knowledge.' Einstein. A genius," he murmured, continuing down the hall.

Too close. Too scary. Arnold is right, Rockett thought, hurrying to the gym. *We've got to find the puppy's owner, pronto. But how? Is there someone who could help who wouldn't blow Jessie's cover?*

Juno would know what to do.

Juno??!! What am I saying? Juno will be here. Tonight. But no way am I asking her for help. She hasn't got a lock on brains in our family.

The sports center was deserted.

Almost.

Someone was crying.

Rockett heard the muffled snuffles as she dashed through the locker room toward the shower stalls.

And there was Nicole.

"Oh, no!" they both screeched at once.

"What are you doing here?" Nicole demanded.

Her face was red and puffy and streaked with runny eye makeup. She had been bending over one of the sinks across from the shower stalls when Rockett walked in. She was glowering at Rockett now, in the mirror. "And why are you wearing that dumb coat?"

"I, uh, um, need to . . . What about you?" Rockett asked. "Are you okay?"

Nicole whirled around. "You're spying on me, aren't you?"

"Why would I do that?" Rockett said, confused.

"Because, like everyone else who wishes they were me in this totally junior high school, Rockett Movado, you would be sooo thrilled to find out that I have . . ." Nicole stopped abruptly, searching for the right word.

"Problems?" Rockett offered.

46

"You wish. No," Nicole insisted. "What I was going to say is that I have the best life of anyone ever. Except, of course, it's not one hundred percent perfect. There just might be one or two thorns in the flawless garden of roses known as me."

"Well, everybody has problems, Nicole."

"Of course they do. To begin with, everybody is not me. Which is a problem right there. Get real, Rockett. What kind of problems would I have?"

Remembering Mavis's words, Rockett said cautiously, "Problems at home?"

Nicole went ballistic.

"Me? My home? *Casa Perfecta*? What could be wrong in paradise with parents like mine? Reginald and Celeste care deeply about me. They live to make me happy. They don't make a move without checking with me first. You think I have problems at home? So not!"

For a moment, Rockett considered backing down, saying, *Hey, it wasn't me, it was Mavis.*

But suddenly Nicole burst into tears.

And Trouble stirred inside his pouch.

Rockett didn't know who to comfort first.

"Don't cry, Nicole. Whatever is going on —"

"I am not crying!" Nicole shouted, startling her. "There's something in my eye!"

Rockett felt Trouble stiffen at the angry voice, then begin to shake and whimper.

"What's that?" Nicole demanded.

"Um, what?" Rockett tried to sound innocent while

47

hugging the pup through Jessie's coat. "I was just clearing my throat."

"Oh, yeah? What did you swallow? A dog?"

"Stop shouting," Rockett warned her. "You're scaring him."

Nicole's mouth fell open. Rockett gasped. In the stunned silence that followed, Trouble's soft whimpering echoed through the tiled room.

"It is a dog," Nicole said, surprised. "You're hiding a dog in that frumpy coat."

Rockett couldn't believe what she'd blurted. "He's homeless," she said softly, opening the coat carefully to show Nicole the puppy.

"Oh, he's so little and sleepy and furry and . . . did you say homeless?" Nicole cocked her head at Trouble, who began to squirm.

"I was just going to get him some water." Slipping the little dog out of the carrier, Rockett walked to the sink. "You can't tell anyone. Please, Nicole."

"Homeless?" Nicole repeated, her face crumpling again.

"We don't know who he belongs to. Jessie found him wandering up near the lake. . . ."

"Homeless," Nicole said again, fighting back tears.

Nicole crying over Trouble? Rockett was blown away. She'd never dreamed Nicole Whittaker would go all emotional over the puppy's plight. How wrong had she been to fear the girl? Nicole was way more compassionate than she'd ever suspected.

"It's okay," Rockett tried to console her. "We're going to find his owner. He won't be homeless —"

"No, but I will," Nicole cried. "My parents. They're moving. Celeste and Reginald are planning to skip town and relocate to some desolate jungle village in No-wheresville. And they haven't even told me yet!"

The puppy was lapping water from the faucet. Rockett held him carefully. Keeping an eye on the little dog, she tried to make sense of what Nicole was saying.

"Me!" Nicole shouted. "Wandering the rain forest. Yes, me — your duly elected class president, head cheerleader, most popular girl in the school. I'm going to have to start all over . . . somewhere else."

"You're moving?" Rockett asked.

Nicole's eyes squinched up suddenly into a fierce glare. "I didn't say that," she asserted. "I don't know what you're talking about."

"But, Nicole," Rockett began, "you just said —"

"What I *do* know, however," Nicole cut her off coldly, "is that you are toting a runty little canine around the school in violation of who knows how many rules and health codes. A homeless dog, at that. One that, if I heard you correctly, was found wandering in a foul and dangerous rural area."

"He was up at the lake, Nicole —"

"I stand corrected. A foul, dangerous, and possibly polluted rural area."

"Nicole. Please. He's just a little lost dog who needs

our help. Please, don't say anything to anyone about him."

"I tell you what," Nicole bargained. "I'll keep your secret if you keep mine."

"Of course I will. Actually," Rockett said, smiling gratefully, "I'm not even sure what yours is."

"Like you'd really like to know," Nicole said sarcastically. "Like you really care."

"I do," Rockett insisted. "If I knew what was upsetting you, maybe I could help. . . ."

"Okay, okay. Here's the deal. I'm bursting with this evil information. I'm going to make myself sick over it. I've already totally trashed my makeup. I've got to tell someone. And it can't be anyone important."

Rockett rolled her eyes. "So that would be me, then? Someone of no consequence?"

"Whatever," Nicole said dismissively. "I'm going to tell. And you're not. *Comprende*? If you say one word to anyone about the news I'm about to impart, I will immediately spill your little secret to the entire school staff. Get it?"

"Got it," Rockett said, drying Trouble's mouth and nose with the sleeve of Jessie's coat and tucking the contented little pup back into the baby carrier.

"Okay, here's the thing," Nicole began, "Reginald, that's my dad, the monstrously successful stockbroker. Well, I just discovered that he's been checking out real estate on-line, in some of the most gruesomely remote areas of the world. My life is over. Obviously, my family

50

is planning to move and has grievously failed to notify me."

She raised her chin defiantly, tossing back her smooth blond hair. "They will, of course. Eventually. And then it's *hasta la vista* to all I've worked for." She ticked off her achievements on her perfectly groomed fingers: "My friends. My exalted social and political position. My proud class presidency. The goodwill of teachers I've sucked up to all year — for nothing. Dissed and dispossessed, I'm being torn from all that is rightfully mine."

"Wow, that's the pits," Rockett said. "I know how you feel. It's terrible to be left out of family decisions. I mean, it's not like they're looking for a new house and not telling me or anything, but my parents did this really whack thing, too. My big sister, Juno, is coming home tomorrow and they're, like, forcing me to make room for her in my private space."

"No!" Nicole gasped. "That is so insensitive."

"That's what I thought," Rockett confessed, "but, well, they did actually ask me if it was all right —"

"Typical guilt ploy, passing the buck, making you responsible for their egregious decision," Nicole affirmed. "But excuse me, I think it was my tragedy we were discussing. The loss of my entire support network."

"But, Nicole, your friends will still be your friends. And there's not a chance you won't make excellent new ones. You're a natural-born leader. People are just drawn to you —"

"Grow up, Rockett," Nicole advised. "Once the secret's

out, I'm history. The minute anyone finds out I'm leaving, I'll be dead girl walking. Before my bags are packed, there'll be a new number-one One, a quick class election, and my cheerleading uniform will be retired to the trophy case. I'm flesh and blood, Rockett. I can't stand the thought of being here yet being ignored."

"Whitney and Stephanie would never ignore you," Rockett said, shocked at the girl's bleak scenario.

"Oh, please." Nicole studied herself in the mirror above the sinks. "If they knew I was leaving, they'd blow me off so fast I'd be picking leaves out of my hair for a year. Don't mistake this for some morbid plunge in self-esteem. I'm a realist. Whit and Steph will do just what I'd do — get over it and move on."

I never thought I'd feel sorry for Nicole, Rockett realized, but I do. I fully know how harsh it is to switch schools, start over, make new friends. But she's way wrong about Stephanie and Whitney. Even though we're apart, Meg, my best bud from my old school, is still my true blue. What would she have felt like if I'd just left without even saying good-bye?

"But you've got to tell them. You can't just disappear. They'll be so hurt."

"How innocent you are," Nicole said coldly, turning her back on Rockett, "but the what-I-should-do part of our chat is so over. Now, what are you going to do with the poky little puppy?" she asked, beginning to repair her makeup.

"Find his owner or get him a new one as fast as possible," Rockett said, making the jarring switch from

Nicole's problem to her own. "A bunch of kids are meeting in the cafeteria to figure out how. Would you be interested in helping us?"

"Not really. I mean, I probably should. Don't I know the heartache of homelessness?" Nicole asked, brushing a fresh dusting of blush onto her cheeks. "Plus, I'm a brutally brilliant problem solver. But let's be real. If your little dog finds a home, how can I be sure you won't rat me out? Sorry, Rockett."

They both froze at the sound of girls filing into the gym.

Next door, the locker room began to echo with noise and laughter.

"Remember what I said," Nicole hissed. "No one knows I'm leaving. No one. That puppy's future is in your hands, Rockett — or should I say, your mouth. Keep your lip zipped or he's history, just one more pathetic little poocheroo in a cold shelter full of needy canines."

Rockett gulped as a muddy gang of younger girls trooped into the shower area. Loud and happy, they were hyped on winning their intramural soccer match.

"Pinch me! It's Nicole Whittaker," a starstruck player exclaimed. "Oh, wow, Nicole, you should have seen us play."

There were excited murmurs all around.

"We were awesome," another girl offered, then shyly added, "I mean, not as awesome as you."

"Don't forget, Rockett," Nicole warned, pulling a pile of photographs out of her quilted designer purse. They were pictures of Nicole in full cheerleading garb. "We never had this little talk."

"What talk?" Rockett replied dutifully on her way out the door.

"Good girl," Nicole said. Then she turned away, graciously agreeing to autograph one of her photos for a fan.

I did it again! I can't believe it. Why in the world did I tell Nicole? And just because she shared her family problem, did I have to unload my own?

I was flattered that Nicole confided in me, that we briefly bonded, that I could so relate to her issues. But now bonding's turned to blackmail. And it's Jessie's butt and Trouble's future that are on the line.

Okay, she promised herself. *That's it. The lip is zipped. No one, absolutely no one else, is going to know.*

CHAPTER SEVEN

Minus her vest, Mavis was pacing the hall in front of Mr. Shuliss's room. As Rockett rushed toward her, Mavis stopped, tapped one clog impatiently on the floor, and elaborately checked her oversized watch.

It didn't take a fortune-teller to read her mood.

"If I waited one more minute I wouldn't even be here," Mavis grumbled. "Jessie took off already for social studies."

"I'm sorry," Rockett said. "I ran into . . ." She stopped herself. "I ran into a little problem, that's all. I'm really sorry, Mavis. Are we all set?"

"Some of us are," Mavis said pointedly. She opened the burlap bag slung across her shoulder. "We put in Jessie's cardigan at the bottom and the stinky-rinky scarf Zeit-nut keeps in his locker. And I donated my very own vest, so it should be extraordinominally cozy. So, er, where's . . . the *package?*" she whispered sinisterly.

The bell rang. Mavis shrieked. Rockett pulled the jumpy girl away from the doorway.

"Here he is." Grateful that the bell hadn't startled Trouble awake, she gently lifted the sleeping pup out of the baby carrier and lowered him into Mavis's bag. Without opening his eyes, he settled with a ruffled sigh into the nest of warm clothing.

"Goggles, goggles, goggles," Mr. Shuliss was droning as they rushed into the lab. "Does everyone have goggles? Today," he said, running a pale hand through his wheat-colored hair, "we will be working with carbon acids."

Rockett climbed onto a stool opposite Whitney. Mavis scrambled to the last empty workstation a row away.

"Who can tell me something about carbon acid? Carbon as in carbon dioxide." Mr. Shuliss wrote CO_2 on the blackboard.

"See-oh-two," he carefully pronounced it, tapping the word with his chalk stick. "For instance," he asked, pacing before the board, "is it stable or unstable?"

"If it's like Max," Cleve murmured, "it's definitely unstable."

A couple of kids laughed. Max just grinned. "If it's like your room, Cleveland, my man," he said, "it's a total stable."

Snickers and murmurs of "Ooooh, he gotcha" and "You're dissed" swept the classroom.

"What's with the outfit, Rockett? Why are you wearing that dumb coat of Jessie's?" Whitney asked.

"Um . . ." She crossed her fingers under the table hoping that whatever popped out of her mouth wouldn't be too lame. "I was cold."

Ugh. Cold was so what she wasn't. If anything, she was starting to sweat. And she couldn't even take off the

56

coat now. The baby carrier was still strapped on underneath, so no chance she was going to cool off in this class.

"I mean, I have a cold. Brrrrr," she said, pretending to shiver. She glanced over at Mavis. Where was her burlap bag?

It was at Mavis's feet. But Mavis seemed to have forgotten all about it.

Mr. Shuliss was oblivious to Max and Cleve's exchange. "Stable or unstable?" he asked again, blinking blankly back at the class. "No one? Well, carbons are unstable. Can anyone give me an example of a common carbon, one you'd find around the house?"

Rockett tried not to be too obvious about watching Mavis's purse. What if Trouble woke? What if he crawled out of the burlap bag? With or without safety goggles, a science lab was no place for a puppy to wander.

But so far the bag hadn't stirred.

"A garage!" From the back of the room, Bo Pezanski shouted out his answer.

Everyone kind of went "Huh?" and stared at him.

"Well, Shuliss said car-barn, didn't he?" Bo smirked.

"An interesting guess, but unfortunately incorrect." Mr. Shuliss broke the news to Bo over the hoots and catcalls of the class. "We're discussing carbons, Mr. Pezanski."

The door opened with a screeching unoiled squeak that silenced the laughter.

"Nicole, come in, come in," Mr. Shuliss said absent-mindedly. "Are you late?"

"I have a perfectly good excuse," Nicole snapped, glancing around the lab for an empty seat.

"Yeah, and she'll tell you what it is as soon as she thinks it up," Max teased.

Nicole froze him with an icy glare. Then, grimacing with distaste, she headed for the last empty stool in the room, opposite Mavis.

"And that perfectly good excuse might be?" Mr. Shuliss asked.

"So personal," Nicole shot back at him.

Passing Rockett's table, she threw a warning look her way, then said to Mr. Shuliss, "Can we talk about this after class, please? I mean, I'm here to learn all about . . ." She checked the blackboard. "Amazing!" she shrieked, clutching her heart. "My absolute favorite subject. Co-two."

"That's C-O-two," Whitney whispered.

"Whatever," Nicole said.

"Safety goggles, Nicole," Mr. Shuliss reminded her, "if you please. There should be a pair in the laminar flow hood —"

Plopping herself onto the stool opposite Mavis, Nicole opened her purse. "Used eyewear? I think not."

She pulled out a pair of Lucite goggles with fire-engine-red frames and waved them at the teacher.

"You're asking me, the adored Nicole Anne Whittaker, whose proud parents cherish her above all else, to wear lenses fingered by science nerds of classes past? No, thanks."

It was lucky the class had been distracted by Nicole's entrance, Rockett thought, because, yes, the burlap bag had begun to move.

"Baking soda. Baking soda is a carbon. While it looks harmless and is, indeed, just a quiet little powder used, predictably enough, in baking, as well as for absorbing refrigerator food odors, chemically it can be volatile or unstable," Mr. Shuliss went on. "What we're going to do today is demonstrate what happens when we try to neutralize or stabilize this volatile carbon.

"I think you'll enjoy this intriguing little experiment. It's simple, nontoxic, possibly the safest volatile chemical reaction we know," he promised blandly, passing out measured packets of baking soda. "Now I want you to divide this baking soda. Each person take half a packet and pour it into your flasks."

He indicated the long glass tubes sitting above Bunsen burners on each table.

But Rockett's eyes were glued to the purse that was moving away from Mavis's feet.

"There you go, girls." Mr. Shuliss gave Rockett a packet.

Without looking up, she accepted the baggie of baking soda from him and mindlessly tore it open.

"Excuse me?" Whitney said, holding out her hand for her portion of the powder.

Rockett didn't hear her. *Was that Trouble's nose peek-*

ing from the burlap purse, she wondered, dumping the entire bag of baking soda into the glass tube on her side of the table.

"That cold's affecting your head. You are too weird today," Whitney decided, dismissing Rockett.

"Now, what neutralizes acids?" Mr. Shuliss asked.

"Alkalines," Mavis contributed as the bulging purse beneath her desk wandered further.

"Exactly. Alkaline neutralizes acid. And in simple household baking soda we have a safe source of alkaline. Thank you, Mavis."

Mavis was swinging her leg. Her clog-clad foot was coming way close to the wriggling bag on the floor, Rockett noticed.

Nicole mimicked Mr. Shuliss sarcastically. "Thank you, Mavis." Whispering loudly enough for her friends to hear, she said, "No fair, no fair, Mr. Shuliss. Mavis cheated. She didn't really know the answer. She was just . . . reading my mind."

Stephanie giggled obligingly.

"I sense your pain, Nicole," Mavis said. "You want to cover it up with nastiness, you can try. But it will still be there — deeeep inside." To Rockett's relief, Mavis's foot stopped bobbing.

"Pain? I don't know what you mean," Nicole protested.

"Yeah, right," Mavis scoffed, unaware that her lumpy purse was inching under her stool.

A shiny wet stub of a nose poked out. It was followed by a pair of curiously blinking brown eyes. Then an ear appeared, bent pinkly back, and another flopped forward, furry and brown.

"Who told you?" Nicole demanded. Her head spun so fast toward Rockett that her hair almost lashed Mavis's cheek.

Instinctively, Rockett looked up, trying to draw attention away from the puppy crawling out of Mavis's purse.

"No one told me anything," Mavis protested smugly. "I read your mind."

Nicole's hands flew to her forehead, as if blocking the view.

"Don't push it," she warned, staring daggers at Mavis.

"Okay, now, class. There's a beaker of vinegar on each desk. Carefully add one teaspoon of vinegar to the baking soda in your flasks . . . and watch what happens when carbons are neutralized."

Nicole turned to Rockett. "Mavis isn't the only one who reads minds around here. I know a certain little secret, too."

That little secret had migrated from under Mavis's stool and was now tugging at the laces of Rockett's sneakers.

Trying to act unconcerned, Rockett dumped the entire beaker of vinegar into the baking soda flask.

"Rockett, don't!" Whitney and Mavis hollered at the

same time. Trouble growled and yipped at the shoelace.

"What was that?!" Stephanie asked, leaning over her table to see what had made the noise.

"That was —" Nicole began.

A terrifying *SHHHHHHUMP!* silenced her.

A tooth-jarring, eye-watering static sound fizzed electrically through the lab, as if a hyper hornet army were getting ready to attack a nest of giant, wired bees.

Rockett and Whitney flew backward off their stools, rushing away from the bubbling, hissing, explosive white mess boiling over the beaker on their worktable.

Nicole led the screaming.

The frothing foam spewed like a geyser.

Hissing and spitting, it slathered the neon lab lights, which sparked and seethed.

It blew like a blizzard, smacked faces, plopped onto heads, stuffed fear-flared nostrils and gaping mouths like hurled mashed potatoes in a food fight.

Rockett fell to her knees and tried to find the puppy in the pandemonium.

She came face-to-face with Mavis, whose kinky hair was flaked with blobs of vinegary baking soda. She was searching furiously through her burlap bag.

"Where's Trouble?" Rockett asked.

"He got away," Mavis reported miserably.

Confession Session

Whoa, dudes, that was a bangin' experiment! Shuliss's class is a royal yawn most of the time, but what a wake-up call today. *Blam!* I'm thinking of switching tracks from breakout computer freak to science geek.

Bo. Is that short for Bonehead or Bozo?

I feel icky about passing the puppy from kid to kid. But no way could I have left him shivering in the woods in the middle of a thunderstorm. I was bummed that Rockett got so many other kids involved. But now I think she did the right thing. It's gonna take more than just the two of us to help Trouble. I hope everyone shows for our lunchtime brainstorming session.

CHAPTER EIGHT

Where was Trouble? The lab floor was filling with water. Somehow the explosion had set off the ceiling sprinklers. Slippery, slimy blobs of baking soda dripped from the tables.

Kids were running and sliding everywhere, splashing around. A couple of glass beakers had rolled off workstations and shattered.

Rockett's stomach was knotted with concern for the little dog.

"What are you doing down there?" Rockett looked up into Whitney's frowning face. "What are you looking for?"

She hated having to lie to Whitney again. Of all The Ones, Rockett felt closest to her. And she knew that, in her cool and distant way, Whitney liked her, too.

But, right now, Whitney was studying her skeptically.

Zip the lip, zip the lip, zip the lip, Rockett chanted to herself. But underneath a voice was saying, *Why don't I just tell the truth? Does it really matter? Nicole already knows. I may as well let Whitney in on it. It would feel so good to stop making up excuses. And then we'd be sharing a secret, one that could bring us closer.*

Right, and totally trash my friendship with Jessie! I mean, what if Whitney's not a pet person? Would she get Jessie and Trouble in more trouble? Do I have the right to risk their welfare to win Whitney's friendship?

Risk Trouble's welfare? What am I thinking? I've already done worse than that!

"Excuse me," Whitney persisted, "I asked what you're looking for."

Rockett had no lies left, only desperation and fear.

"I . . . I dropped my glasses," Mavis improvised wildly.

"The ones you're wearing?" Whitney asked, arms folded across her chest.

"No. I mean, yes. I mean goggles," the flustered psychic stammered.

Rockett sighed. She was way beyond frantic now. She'd hit rock bottom, she decided. Literally. Here she was on her hands and knees, on the science lab floor, in a mess of exploded baking soda. She'd spent the entire morning plotting and scheming, running, hiding, lying — and she hadn't managed to help Jessie or protect Trouble.

"We're looking for a puppy," she told Whitney wearily. "I was hiding it under this coat before class." She lifted the garment's soaked hem and wrung it out dejectedly.

"It got loose and crawled out of Mavis's bag just before the big bang. Which was all my fault. All of it. The blast, the lost little dog. He must be so afraid and alone. I don't care what happens to me. I'd take a year's worth of detention if I could find that poor puppy."

Whitney knelt down beside them. "I think," she said, showing them the soaked and shaking creature she'd been cradling, "if you blow-dry this drowned dust mop, it might fluff up into an actual dog."

"Trouble!" Rockett exclaimed, rearing up so suddenly she banged her head on the desktop.

"Are you sure?" Mavis asked, studying the drenched puppy. "It looks more like a hamster."

"Perfect!" Rockett said. "That's what we'll say if we bump into Mrs. Herrera. That we're rescuing the class hamster. Let's get him out of here, fast."

"I'll go with you," Whitney volunteered, reluctant to let go of the shivering puppy.

"Trouble? Is that his name?" she asked as they raced from the room. "What a total cutie-patootie he is!"

Reviving Trouble was no problem. The little dog loved the warm breeze of the girls' room hand dryer and squirmed and yipped happily in Rockett's hands.

With classes still in session, the bathroom was deserted. Mavis stood guard outside anyway.

Whitney got out the hair pick she used on her long, thick, curly mane. "Hand him over," she urged Rockett. "I'll style him. He is majorly cute. But what are you going to do with him next period?"

"If he were a fish, we could stow him in Mavis's bag. But it's totally soaked. Is there any way you could watch him?" Rockett tried not to sound too desperate.

"I wish. I've got computer lab with Ms. Chen. Anyway, where would I keep him? I mean, I'd even do the baby carrier thing and wear that random coat, except that it's dripping wet."

"Well, yeah, the hem is," Rockett admitted. Then she laughed. "And anyway, someone would probably ask why *you're* wearing it."

"You want to know what I thought?" Whitney was gently picking out the little dog's shiny coat, fluffing his dark, curly fur. "I thought you and Jessie had some secret club going and that the coat was like an initiation stunt or something."

"Wow, that's so cool. I wish I'd thought of that," Rockett said. "Seriously, Whitney, it's a choice excuse. Only I've got PE next period and I can't play soccer in a wet wool coat. What if I could get the hem dry? Could you wear it then?"

"And pretend I'm in a club with you and Jessie?" Whitney looked doubtful. "Nicole would be all over me like jelly on peanut butter. She'd flip out."

Rockett's shoulders sagged. "Definitely," she agreed.

"Of course," Whitney added, rubbing noses with Trouble, "Nicole's not in my computer class."

"It would just be for one period," Rockett assured her, starting to unfasten the baby carrier. "And then we'll all meet to figure out how to get him back to his owner."

It might really work, she thought with a rush of hope and adrenaline. With Whitney on board and Trouble safe again, anything was possible. All of a sudden, having a gazillion kids in on Jessie's "secret" didn't seem whack at all. It just meant more help, more ideas, more people working together to get the little guy back home.

The bathroom door opened. "Nicole and Stephanie coming this way," Mavis warned them. "We've gotta hide Trouble."

"I am so outta here," Whitney said, handing the happily panting pup back to Rockett.

"I understand," Rockett said, hopes crashing. She scrambled to tie the carrier strap around her waist again.

"Turn around. I'll do it," Whitney offered. "You know what, you guys just duck into a stall with him. I'll get rid of them."

Rockett barely had time to return the puppy to the warm, dry pouch and squeeze into a stall with Mavis before the bathroom door banged open.

"So this is where you've been hiding," Nicole announced.

"Hiding?" Whitney said weakly. "Why would I hide?"

"She's kinda upset," Stephanie told Whitney.

"Kinda upset?" Nicole sighed. "Hello. My life is at a crossroads here. Tissue. Tissue!" She snapped her fingers at them.

"Nic, why won't you tell us what's wrong?" Whitney asked as Stephanie popped into the stall next to Rockett's, hunting for tissue paper for her bud.

What if there's no paper? Will Stephanie bust into our hiding place and find me standing on a toilet seat, in a wet overcoat, hanging on to Mavis for balance?

69

Rockett shut her eyes.

How lame, she told herself. *Like this is gonna make me invisible instead of blind.*

Then, with a rush of relief, she heard Nicole blow her nose.

"I can't tell you. You can't do anything about it," she said, snuffling. "I just came in here for a moment's solitude. I need to be alone."

"But, Nic, you begged me to come with you," Stephanie protested.

"Not that I didn't want to be with you. I'm dying to find out . . . I mean, I'm dying to comfort and console you — and I so would, if only I knew what the problem was."

"Mavis was right," Nicole said miserably. "That little wash-and-wear weasel was so on the money when she spoke of pain."

Rockett put her finger to her lips warning Mavis, whose eyes were all scrunched up in outrage, to stay quiet.

"Nic," Whitney said, as if she'd just had the best idea in the world, "what's the best cure for pain? Pleasure. And what's our greatest pleasure?"

"Makeovers at the mall?" Nicole asked.

"After that."

"Oh, I know. I know," Stephanie offered excitedly. "Being the center of attention!"

"Totally," Whitney said. "And here we are in a dreary bathroom where no one can see us."

"Let's go where the action is and flaunt ourselves," Nicole decided.

"Excellent!" Whitney put her arms though theirs and led them out of the girls' room.

"Whew." Rockett climbed down from the seat. "That was too close."

"Way too close — to Nicole," Mavis fumed. "Weasel? Well, she can't *weasel* out of the fact that I was fully corrective about her distress. The tingle never lies. Mavis rules!"

"You so called it right," Rockett agreed.

"Help me with the hem of Jessie's coat. Can you hold it under the dryer while I'm wearing it?"

Mavis could and did. But in the time before the bell rang, the best they managed was to warm it from sopping wet to merely damp.

"Five minutes till next period and I have no idea what we'll do with him," Rockett said in a blue funk.

The bathroom door flew open. It was Whitney, huffing and puffing. "I just ran over from the gym. Nicole and Steph are in PE with you. Give me the carrier, the coat, and Trouble," she said. "I'll meet you in the cafeteria next period."

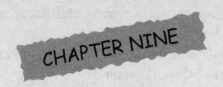

CHAPTER NINE

Mavis and Arnold were glaring at each other from opposite ends of a cafeteria table an hour later when the CSGs and Jessie arrived, looking for Rockett.

"Reserved?" Jessie read the folded sheet of paper Arnold had propped up on the table.

"Get real, Zitbomb." Dana laughed. "Quarantined is more like it. Are you two honestly expecting crowds to mob you?"

"Are you here for the meeting?" Mavis cut Dana short.

"The one about you-know-who," Nakili ventured cautiously.

"Jessie's foster pup," Miko said.

"I never thought of it that way. That is so cool." Jessie beamed.

"Yuck!" Dana looked disgustedly at Arnold's tray, in the center of which was a plate heaped high with slabs of steaming undercooked meat loaf, gummy mashed potatoes, and broccoli boiled bark brown.

"It's Mr. Pill's Monday special," he said defensively.

"Yeah, and Tuesday's special will be served in the hospital." Sharla cruised over and set down her soda and chips. "Where's our furry little guest of honor?"

"Who invited you?" Dana demanded.

"I did," Rockett said, surprised and happy to see Sharla among the gathered group.

Sharla examined her chipped nail polish. "Yeah, well, I had time to kill. Where's the mutt?" she asked.

"In computer lab, I think," Rockett answered, grinning, "or on his way here. We've really got some work to do. It's getting harder and harder to hide him."

"I can't believe you're gonna eat that," Dana said, shaking her head at Rockett's tray.

"Let it go, Dana," Miko admonished her bud.

"It's not for me, it's for Trouble," Rockett explained.

"Did someone call my name?"

Rockett turned to see Ruben strolling her way, flanked by Cleve and Max.

"Hey, guys," Nakili greeted them. Then she looked questioningly at Rockett as if to say, *Do they know?*

Ruben answered her unspoken question. "Greetings. I brought along a couple of *amigos* interested in animal rights," he said, jerking a thumb at Cleve and Max.

"Yeah, that's 'cause they're animals," Stephanie said, walking up.

Jessie looked at Rockett nervously. "Stephanie? Um, er, hi, Stephanie," she said. "What are you doing here?"

"Rockett invited Nicole, and Nic sent me," Stephanie answered.

"Nicole knows?" Miko asked, setting down her tray and sliding onto the molded-plastic bench attached to the table.

"Is she coming?" Rockett asked Stephanie.

"She's still making up her mind. Something's up with the girl."

"Who are you talking about?" Whitney asked, joining them. "Nicole?"

"Excuse me? What's that you're wearing?" Stephanie quizzed, hands on her hips.

"Is that my coat?" Jessie asked, clearly surprised to see Whitney wearing it. "What happened to the bottom?"

Ruben laughed. "Didn't you hear? Rockett blew up the science lab."

"And set off the sprinklers," Max said.

"Oh, no! That was you?" Miko covered her mouth, trying to hide her giggles.

"I'm sorry, Jess," Rockett said sheepishly. "The coat got kinda wet."

"Man, you should have seen it. It was beautiful!" Cleve and Max high-fived each other. "Chronic, man. Jammin'."

"Shhhhh. You'll wake him," Whitney scolded, holding the coat closed.

It was the wrong thing to say. Everyone turned toward her, mobbed her, and started talking at once.

"Him?" Stephanie asked. "You mean the puppy? Where is he?"

"How'd he do in computer lab?" Mavis asked.

"Probably better than you, Warts-ella." Arnold laughed, honking like a donkey at his own joke.

"Ooo, where's my itty-bitty puppy-poo?" Dana cooed.

"Is he in the baby carrier?" Jessie asked.

"Yeah, there he is. I see him," Cleve said excitedly. "Max, look at the little dude all curled up in that sling Whitney's wearing."

"What is that thing?" Max asked.

"A baby carrier," Jessie told him, embarrassed. "It was all I could think of. I found it out in the garage last night. It used to be mine."

"Let me see him, I can't see him." Nakili hopped at the edge of the crew surrounding Whitney.

"Back off, back off!" Suddenly Sharla pushed her way to the front. "You guys are supposed to be helping this poor little mutt." Arms flung out protectively, she stationed herself in front of Whitney. "Not scaring him to death."

Whew, I am so majorly psyched. I can hardly believe this is happening. Everyone showed! Everyone but Nicole. The CSGs are working with The Ones. Arnold and Mavis, who can't stand each other, are trying to solve the same problem. Ruben, Cleve, and Max, our big-time class clowns, are acting serious about saving the puppy. And here's Sharla, who'd probably call Jessie a wimp, totally protecting the little lost dog Jessie risked everything to rescue. Trouble ought to get a Nobel Peace Prize for bringing so many different kids together.

"Sharla's right," Rockett said. "We don't have a whole lot of time. Let's sit down and figure out what to do, okay?"

"Please," Jessie added meekly. "I can't take him home again. My mom'll throw a fit if he knocks anything over or, like, ruins her equipment."

"I'll take him," Dana volunteered.

75

"We've got soccer practice," Stephanie reminded her.

"Oh, yeah. And then I want to go to the mall. And anyway, what if Marlo gets jealous?" She sat down next to Miko and Nakili. "Nope. I pass. It's not gonna work."

"Can we move on?" Sharla said. "Like what are you all gonna do about finding him a real home?"

"I think we should search for his owner first," Jessie said. "If he were my dog, I'd be worried sick and want him back so bad."

"Can't we do both?" Rockett asked.

"Definitely," Ruben backed her. "We can try to trace his owner and start looking for a place he can stay right away."

"Like a foster home," Jessie said. "But how?"

"We could make flyers," Nakili suggested.

"All right." Mavis had appointed herself secretary. "Nakili's in favor of flyers."

Miko seconded the idea. "Flyers and posters. And we could put a notice in the school paper."

"Nobody's gonna care without a reward," Dana decided.

"Flyers, posters, newspaper notices?" Sharla shook her head. "You people are pitiful. That'll really turn up his owner — in a year or two."

"Excuse me. Hello? I'm here," a sharp, determined voice announced.

Rockett looked up to find Nicole impatiently surveying the table. At her side, a nervous seventh grader was struggling to balance two full cafeteria trays.

"Nic!" Stephanie cried out happily. "You made it. Oh, I knew you would. And just in time. We were getting way bogged down in negativity." She glanced meaningfully at Sharla. "And we, like, so need positive input."

"You're looking for something positive from Nicole?" Sharla snorted scornfully. "Give her a rabies test. That'll come out positive."

Nicole ignored her. "Positive input about what?" she wanted to know.

"About finding a home," Jessie began, "for —"

With a gasp, Nicole cut her off. "A home? Who's looking for a home? Not my parents." She whirled toward Rockett then. "Has someone risked all they hold dear by heinously betraying a friend's desperate secret?" she hissed.

"What secret?" Stephanie asked.

"We're talking about the puppy, Nicole," Whitney said. "We're trying to find a home for Trouble."

"Oh," Nicole said. "And, excuse me, Whitney, but what are you doing in that creepy coat?"

"She's hiding the puppy," Jessie whispered.

The seventh grader at Nicole's side was shifting uncomfortably from foot to foot. "Um, Nicole, can I put your tray down now?" she asked cautiously.

"If someone will make room for me!" Nicole glared at Whitney and Stephanie.

Stephanie squeezed over. Pushing her lunch tray out of the way and mashing Dana into Arnold, she generously patted the space she'd vacated.

Unconcerned, Nicole slid onto the bench and snapped her fingers. Her helper gratefully set down her tray and rushed off.

Dana leaned forward. "I'd never have guessed you were an animal lover," she challenged Nicole.

"She's not, her mom is," Max teased. "She loves wearing them, right, Nic?"

"Oh, my mom, too," Dana said sarcastically.

"I've seen your mom," Nicole said coldly. "What's she doing, breeding polyesters?"

"Nic, don't," Whitney scolded.

"What's Nic so flipped about?" Cleve asked.

"She refuses to talk about it," Stephanie said. "I mean, how can we help if she won't tell us?"

"Maybe her favorite manicurist quit. Forget her," Sharla advised. "I mean, what kind of problem could La Whittaker have, anyway?"

Rockett forced herself to sit still. She wanted to race after Nicole. She wanted to comfort the girl. She wanted to try to talk her into opening up, filling her friends in on her secret. Now Whitney and Stephanie were hurting, too.

Sharla cleared her throat. Rockett looked up and saw Sharla checking her out.

Her head was tilted as she studied Rockett with undisguised curiosity. Her expression, a thoughtful smirk, all but said, *Give, girl. What do you know about Nicole that even her best friends don't?*

Rockett looked away.

"As I was saying before Nicole staged her hissy fit," Sharla said after a moment, "flyers and posters are gonna take way too long."

"She's right," Mavis observed. "They will take time."

"Yeah," Ruben agreed. "First we gotta make them, then plaster them all over the 'hood —"

"And up at the lake, where Jessie found him," Miko added. "Gee, I didn't think of that."

"Yeah, and even if we put a notice in the school paper, it won't come out until next week," Nakili noted.

"Where're you gonna stash the mutt all that time?" Sharla challenged. "Unless, of course, you" — she looked at Whitney — "are planning on wearing a moldy coat for the rest of the term."

"I'm just holding him for now," Whitney insisted. "Rockett, you promised. It was just for one period."

Rockett's head was spinning. Part of her was still with Nicole, worrying and fretting about the girl. Part of her was wondering what Sharla's look had really meant. But mostly she was amazed, elated, psyched, and awestruck at how many kids had actually gathered to help Jessie and Trouble.

"How about the Internet?" Arnold asked. "We could conduct a cybersearch. Post a notice on the Web. Design a Web site for a dog in distress."

"Yes!" Suddenly Rockett wished Arnold were Ruben Rosales so she could kiss him for being so smart. "And we could do that right away. Can you handle it, Arnold?"

"To rescue a needy pooch, fair maiden? Certainly," he

said. "Well, sort of. I'm not exactly one hundred percent sure of how to do it."

"And what would it say?" Whitney asked.

"Whatever the words are, it's got to be well-designed," Miko pointed out. "A real attention grabber."

"Can we post the pup's picture on the Net?" Cleve asked. "He's way cool-lookin'."

"Yeah, and then someone might recognize him," Max added.

"Do we have a picture of him?" Miko asked.

"No, but I could borrow a camera from the art department," Rockett volunteered. "I'm sure Mr. Rarebit would lend me one."

"Do they have a Polaroid?" Ruben said. "We need this fast, right?"

"Can we design a site by tonight?" Nakili wondered.

"With Zeit-weed in charge? Ha. Don't bet on it," Mavis snorted.

"Whoa, whoa, whoa." Arnold raised his hands. "I may be super, but I'm not supernatural. Even an intrepid knight such as I can't write and design a site, scan a photo onto the Net, *and* attend my next three classes. I mean, who could?"

Juno, Rockett thought. *Omigosh, Juno could so do it. My brilliant problem-solving sister, the computer graphics major. She knows how to scan art into her computer. She could design something that would rate major attention.*

"Juno!" Jessie shrieked. "Rockett, didn't you say your

sister, Juno, was this cyber-genius with great design skills?"

"No," Rockett said. "I mean, yes. I mean, she could do it. Probably. But she's in college, Jess. If you think Arnold's busy, imagine what Juno's got to do. I can't ask her."

You mean won't, Rockett got real with herself. *Will not. No way. Like never.*

Sharla stood up suddenly. "Well, it's been boring," she said. Flinging her purse over her shoulder, she walked around the table to Rockett's side. "Got a minute?" she asked. "I got something to say to you. Alone."

Rockett excused herself. "I'll be right back," she said, then followed Sharla to a deserted corner of the cafeteria.

"What's up?" she asked. "What did you want to talk to me about?"

"A trade-off," Sharla said. "You want someone to baby-sit the mutt overnight, right?"

"Are you going to do it?" Rockett was hyper with hope again.

"Sure. Why not? My moms is on the late shift at the bowling alley this month. The little runt can keep me company."

"I can't believe it. Sharla, that's so cool. And you like him, don't you? I saw it when you were holding him. You were so good with him. You're a natural."

"Hold on there, homey. I said a trade, right? I'll take

the pup tonight. I'll even keep him till you find his owner —"

"You are so the best!" Rockett blurted out enthusiastically.

Sharla smiled her wolfish grin. "But only if you tell me what's up with Nicole."

Rockett's shoulders sagged. Her heart fell. "Why?" she managed to ask. "I mean, why do you want to know?"

"'Cause I'm a huge fan of the pampered princess." Sharla said. "Listen, I know how Nicole feels about me. Not that I care. I guess from her high horse, everyone looks small and insignificant. And boy, would it be sweet to see her tumble. Call me Mavis, but I sense something. I smell it. The scent of Loser is coming off Nicole Anne Whittaker in waves today. And I think you know why. It's your move, Rockett. What's it gonna be?"

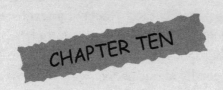

CHAPTER TEN

Rockett felt dumb and deflated, like a bike tire punctured by Sharla's sharpness and leaking air fast.

"I can't," she finally said, her voice breaking embarrassingly.

"No prob." Sharla shrugged. "Your loss," she said, and stalked out of the cafeteria.

Blew that one big-time. Rockett shook her head. *I thought Sharla really cared about Trouble. I was so sure of it. It would've been way beyond cool to have her foster-parent him until we could find his owner. I just didn't count on her hating Nicole more than she loved the pup. But no way am I going to sell out Nicole. She's hurting bad right now. I know how hard family issues can be. And Trouble could be in bigger trouble if I breathe a word.*

Yuck. How could I have been so wrong about Sharla? Juno wouldn't have been. She's so good with people. No wonder everyone's always asking her advice. I can't believe I ever thought Sharla was a s'more, that she had a marshmallow middle — all sweet, soft, and fluffy inside.

What's weird is . . . I still think it's true. But she's so unpredictable.

"What did you say to Sharla Rae that made her take off like that?" Ruben asked, sauntering toward her.

"It's what I didn't say," Rockett answered somberly.

Ruben laughed. "She bummed you, huh?"

"It's not her fault. It's me. It's like I'm so stupid sometimes — especially about people."

"That's true. You are."

That got her attention. Rockett just hoped the misery bubbling inside her didn't boil over into tears.

But Ruben was still smiling.

"Do you really believe that?" he finished his thought. "You're not stupid about people. Look how you got everyone to sit down together today — on *meat loaf* day, too."

Rockett shrugged. Then she blurted out what was really on her mind. "Yeah, but someone like my sister would've gotten us to come up with a solution, which I blew bigtime. There's still no one to watch Trouble."

"Your sister?"

"Juno. Jessie mentioned her before — the computer graphics genius." She sounded really ripe, she thought, sullen and oozing self-pity, but she couldn't stop. "When she's home the phone never stops ringing. Even my folks think she's all that. They practically worship her. She's the kind of person people really trust —"

"Trust me on this," Ruben said. "Whatever happened between you two, it'll work out."

"Between me and Juno? What do you mean?" Rockett asked defensively.

"I was talking about you and Sharla. Whew, she really must've rattled your cage."

"Who, Sharla?"

"No, your sister, what's-her-name? The genius."

"Juno," Rockett said, trying to keep up with Ruben. "She is a genius, really. I mean, about computers and graphic design and about people, too. I guess that's why she's so popular. Because she's way bright and creative and helpful."

"That's what I'm saying. She sounds just like you."

Rockett let herself smile.

"There you go," he said. "So is she really too busy to help you out? Your sister," he clarified. "I mean, when Jessie mentioned her, you nuked the notion in record time."

"Well, she is in college. And she does have a full load of courses," Rockett said uneasily.

"So it's, like, hard to get a hold of her, right?"

"Um, yeah. Usually —"

Ruben cocked his head. "And?" he prompted. "You sounded like you were going to say something else."

Rockett was embarrassed. "Actually, she's coming home for a couple of days. She's staying in my room tonight."

"Tonight?" Ruben made claws of his big hands and, waving them in her face, started humming spooky movie music. "Miracle or coincidence?" he asked in a sinister voice. Then he laughed. "Well, that'll make her really easy to reach."

"I guess," Rockett said, and then she laughed, too.

Miracle or coincidence? Wow. I never looked at it that way. To me it's more about having to clean up my room, stash my fave projects, forget about using the telephone, and listen to everyone quizzing my sister about her honor-roll life.

I mean, Juno is the problem, not the solution, right?

Or is it possible that she isn't showing up to ruin my life but to help me save a desperate, innocent puppy?

Miracle or coincidence?

No way. Too weird. Who'd believe a thing like that — besides Mavis, of course?

"So you ready for English now? I am," Ruben said.

He reached inside his sweatshirt and pulled out a couple of wrinkled, folded pages that had been stashed in his shirt pocket. "Got a decent essay right here, if I do say so myself."

"Mine's in my backpack," Rockett said. "Whoops, I left it at the table. I've got to run over there and get it."

Jessie was waiting. "Rockett," she said, "there's no one who can watch the puppy next period. I've got gym and I'm not going to stash him in my locker. Any ideas?"

Rockett turned to Ruben.

What she saw was a hottie wearing an oversized hooded sweatshirt that could hide a baby carrier every bit as well as Jessie's coat.

Jessie's worried frown broke into a huge grin. "Ruben! You are so cool. The total bomb."

"Yeah, Rube, you the iceman, dude," Cleve cracked.

"The bomb fer sure, man," Max teased.

"That's it. That big fat sweatshirt," Jessie realized. "Omigosh, it's perfect."

"I don't even want to know for what," Ruben insisted. "But I'm glad you *chicas* are into my barrio styling."

"Ruben, the baby carrier will fit inside your sweatshirt," Rockett explained.

The laughing boy's mouth went slack as he digested the information. "A baby carrier?" he said when he could speak again.

"You're asking me to puppy-sit in Ms. Tinydahl's class?" Ruben laughed. "She's on my back all the time anyway about sloppy papers, lost assignments —"

"Didn't you say I know about people?" Rockett asked. "Well, I know about you. You wouldn't let some poor little dog wind up in the pound."

"Are you kidding? If he survived Pill's meat loaf, he can survive anything," Max insisted.

"Even a ride in a sweatshirt." Suddenly Whitney was up, circling Ruben, checking his outfit.

"Aw, go on," Max urged, "do it. I think you should do it."

"Yeah, me too," Cleve chimed in. "Trouble's a bro, man. Okay, he's a little furry runty bro, but he deserves a shot."

Mavis pushed through the crew surrounding Ruben. "Give him a minute or more that he needs. My goose bumps are fail-proof positive."

"On what planet does that mean something?" Dana demanded.

"If you're saying I'm the bonehead who's gonna wear a puppy to English class —" Ruben grinned then winked at Rockett. "Your goose bumps are right, Mavis. Strap on the dog."

"I knew it. I knew you'd do it," Rockett cheered.

Max and Cleve pounded Ruben's back. "Way to go, dude," Cleve said.

"You the man," Max exclaimed.

"It's easy, Ruben. He's not heavy at all," Whitney encouraged, as Stephanie untied the baby carrier and Miko gently held the front of the sling in which Trouble had fallen asleep again, after gorging on warm milk and meat loaf.

"Congratulations." Mavis frantically pumped his hand.

"Ruben rules," Nakili announced. "We'll screen you while you tie on the carrier."

"Ruben gonna take good care of my sugar-booger baby boy, yes he is," Dana crooned as Miko passed the pup-loaded carrier to him.

It was all coming together. Everyone was involved and psyched and pitching in. Except for Arnold, Rockett realized. Where was the boy?

She craned her neck, trying to see past Cleve and Max, and spotted him still sitting at their reserved table, alone.

One of his hands raked his mouse-brown mop of hair, and the other propped up his thin chin. He was bent over his notebook, the one with fantasy holograms and glittery video game stickers all over the cover. A yellow pencil, like a pirate's dagger, was clamped between his teeth.

Rockett walked over to the table. "Did you hear? Ruben's watching Trouble next period."

"Whoopee," Arnold said glumly.

"What's up?" she asked, glancing down at his notebook.

The page was full of squiggles — arrows and circles and starbursts. There were words, too, just a few of them, written in big, block letters and punctuated with question marks. LOST?? REWARD??? and BROWN? she read, before Arnold suddenly slammed the book shut.

"Nothing a first-form warrior couldn't work out," he answered her. "How's your sister?"

"My sister?"

"The bright one Jessie was talking about," he said. "The computer queen. Love to meet her sometime. Soon, I hope. Like today."

"You want to meet my sister?" Rockett asked, perplexed.

"Did I say that?" Arnold laughed nervously. "Naw. Just jesting. I'm cool. I can handle this thing."

"Handle what? Is it about the puppy?" she guessed. "Are you having trouble figuring out what we should do first?"

"I, having trouble?" Arnold objected. "You're talking to Sir Cyber-lot, knight of the Net. Of course, it's true that I'm only your basic overachieving eighth-grade Web master, not a college-level computer graphics major who could probably do a bang-up job designing a truly eye-catching site."

"Like Juno, for instance?" Rockett said softly.

"Juno? Is that your sister?"

"Yes," she said.

"Then, yes. Like Juno, for instance."

"You think maybe I should give her call? Ask her to —"

"Advise us?" Arnold said quickly, his little eyes suddenly alive behind his glasses. "Gee, I don't know. I guess it wouldn't hurt. What the heck? Why not?"

"Yeah," Rockett said weakly, "why not?"

"You all set for class?" Ruben called to her. "Got your essay?"

"Right here," she answered.

Grabbing the backpack she'd left on the bench next to Arnold, she hurried to catch up with Ruben. She would owe him big-time for helping with Trouble.

His sweatshirt was zipped almost all the way up. It was huge and bulky. The three-pound puppy he was carrying underneath it barely made a wrinkle in the loose fabric.

If Trouble just slept through English, no one would notice a thing, Rockett told herself as they approached the classroom.

"Well, well, look who's got the mutt."

Nothing escaped Sharla's X-ray eyes. She was waiting at Ms. Tinydahl's door. Rockett had totally blanked on their having English together.

"Ruben Rosales, dog-sitter. How'd they rope you into it?"

"Hey, Sharla," Ruben said easily. "It's just for this period. Is it really all that noticeable?"

"Naw." Sharla laughed. "I've just never seen your sweatshirt zipped unless it's thirty below."

Ms. Tinydahl came to the door. "In, in, in," she said. "Take your seats. Let's get started."

"Don't you believe that 'just for one period' stuff, either," Sharla advised Ruben, following him inside. "They'll try to sucker you into adopting the little bag of bones."

"Sharla," Rockett began, wanting to apologize — although she wasn't sure for what.

"Save it," Sharla snarled over her shoulder, "for someone who cares. Like your good buddy over there."

She jerked her head toward Nicole, who was rummaging through the books on her desk, trying to find her homework, Rockett guessed.

She was sitting up even straighter than usual, looking defiantly confident despite the traces of tear-streaked mascara under her eyes.

"Hi," Rockett said, taking her seat next to Nicole. "Feeling better?"

"About what?" Nicole snapped, scrunching her eyes at Rockett, daring her to mention the forbidden topic.

"I was just asking," Rockett whispered lamely.

"Oh, and I was just asking, where's that cute little rabies dispenser of yours?"

Behind them, Rockett could hear Sharla snickering. Then Ruben went, "Oh, no!"

Sharla leaned forward and whispered to Nicole, "Does that answer your question?"

"Quiet down, please. Ruben, is something wrong?" Ms. Tinydahl wanted to know.

"No, ma'am. Just got an itch."

Rockett turned to see him smiling stiffly, his hand inside his sweatshirt.

Uh-oh, she thought. *Trouble's awake*.

Then she remembered that Ruben's essay was in his shirt pocket. Maybe the pup was still zoned. Maybe Ruben had just been trying to get his homework.

Pacing at the front of the room, Ms. Tinydahl began to explain the importance of the assignment they were handing in. "So I'm expecting neat, clean, readable papers today. Carefully thought-out and clearly expressed," she concluded. "Problems? Questions?"

Nicole's hand flew up. "I don't have mine. I must've left it home . . . home," she repeated, her lower lip quivering slightly.

"You left your essay at home?" the English teacher asked.

"Hello, are someone's little ears suffering from waxy yellow buildup? Yes, Ms. Tinydahl. I said home! I had, like, this monster traumatic experience this morning. A bitterly life-altering event. And I'm sooooo sorry that I left the only home I've ever known, a chronic mansion, without going, 'Whoops, Ms. Tinydahl's gonna get brutally bent out of shape if I don't run right back up those marble stairs to my vast, way decent room and grab the excellent essay I cranked last night.'"

"What you're saying, then, Nicole," Ms. Tinydahl said calmly, "is that you're unprepared?"

"Unprepared? Oh, yes, Ms. Tinydahl, you could say that. I am heinously unprepared. As unprepared as a trusting girl can be."

Nicole threw her head down onto her desk.

"Whew," Sharla cried admiringly.

"We'll discuss this after class, Nicole," Ms. Tinydahl decided. "All right, then." She started up the aisle, collecting the homework.

"Ruben?" Rockett heard Mrs. Tinydahl say. She turned quickly. Ruben was holding out his hands. They were empty.

"I'm sorry, Ms. Tinydahl," he said.

"Did you leave your work at home, too?" the English teacher asked cautiously.

"No, ma'am," Ruben asserted. "I brought it. And it was good, too. I worked on it for two days. Trust me, it was a winner."

"I'm afraid it's going to take a little more than trust," Ms. Tinydahl said. "What happened?"

Ruben reached inside his sweatshirt and pulled out a small, wrinkled, ripped, soaking-wet piece of paper. "You are so not gonna believe this," he said.

"Try me," Ms. Tinydahl urged.

"The dog ate my homework."

93

Ms. Tinydahl closed her eyes for a moment and massaged her forehead. "Now, where have I heard that before?" she asked, walking past Ruben, not even bothering to examine what was left of his essay.

Sharla cracked up. "I love that little mischief maker," she confided to Rockett.

"Who, Ruben?"

"Naw," Sharla said. "Trouble. What a cool little guy."

"I guess you wouldn't consider — ?"

"We'll talk," Sharla promised. "Right after the bell. I don't want to miss anything. This is, like, the best English class I've ever sat through in my life."

Confession Session

I hope Rockett comes through. I've got a soft spot in my heart for that puppy. He's as cute as Mr. Davis, the teddy bear I've slept with since I was two. I really want to take him home. And I've got a soft spot in my *head* for Nicole the Troll. We've got a lot in common. She's gutsy, pushy, won't bow down, won't take grief. I'd love to do her a solid. Especially since it would radically creep her out to owe me!

My secret is so bringing me down. I'm brutally busting to share it with my bests. But what if they laugh at my rancid luck, instantly quit sucking up to me, turn their backs before my bags are even packed? Misfortune is so unattractive. Rockett thinks I ought to tell them. Could that trivial little carrottop be right?

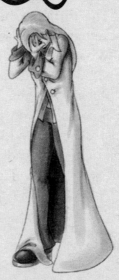

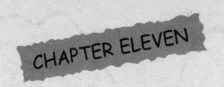

CHAPTER ELEVEN

"Are you mad at me?" Rockett asked Ruben as they walked out of class together. Her fave eighth-grade boy looked seriously bummed. "I'm really sorry Trouble chewed up your paper."

"It's on my PC. I can print out another copy," he said.

"You just gotta know how to handle him." Sharla caught up with them.

"Some puppy things don't just get 'handled,' Sharla," Ruben grumbled. "My paper's not the only thing messed up. No biggie. I probably have a T-shirt or something I can change into in my locker. This one's kinda wet. And so's the baby-thingy."

"The carrier? Oh, wow. I'm, like, so sorry, Ruben." Rockett apologized again as Sharla hooted with laughter.

"What happened?" Jessie asked, hurrying toward them. "Where's Trouble?"

"Ruben's got him," Rockett said.

"So what're you gonna do with him now?" Sharla asked. "You got nothing to hold him in, no place to hide him, right? You ready to do that deal?"

"I can't, Sharla. I gave Nicole my word," Rockett said.

"And don't you forget it!" Nicole was suddenly at their side. "Pretend you don't see me. I nearly bumped into Steph and Whitney a minute ago, and I so can't face them," she confided. Blinking back tears, she fled down the hall.

"What's going on?" Jessie asked.

"Yeah, you gotta fill me in," Sharla insisted. "What's going down with that girl? Who knows, maybe I could help her out."

"You'd help Nicole?" Rockett asked, stunned.

"Why, you think all I want to do is diss her, gloat over the Empress of Ego's problems?" Sharla asked indignantly. "I got a heart. I got a brain. I got a wild imagination. Like, imagine this: how Nicole would feel if I was the one who came to her rescue." Sharla cackled wildly. "Nicole Whittaker at the mercy of Sharla Rae Norvell."

"Listen, I've got to get to my locker and change," Ruben said. "What do I do with the puppy? Who gets him next?"

Rockett looked at Jessie, who shrugged sadly. She had no answer. They were fresh out of options.

"Last chance," Sharla said.

Rockett wanted to give in so badly she didn't trust herself to speak. *Aside from putting Trouble and Jessie in fierce jeopardy, how would I feel if Nicole spread my family issues all over school?* Sighing, she shook her head no.

"You guys are such lame Barneys. Over here, over here," Sharla said gruffly. "I'll hang on to the pathetic mutt. We got art with Mr. Rarebit, right, Rockett? So I'll work on my independent project. Rarebit'll let me go outside if I tell him I want to draw from real life. I mean, face it, what's more depressing than real life?"

"You'll take him?" Jessie couldn't believe it.

"No strings attached?" Rockett asked.

"Well, I could use a leash, but no, not the strings you're talking about," Sharla said. "Come on, Ruben. Let's find someplace to make the switch."

"I'll go with you guys to help," Jessie volunteered.

"Ruben, thanks," Rockett said. "I really appreciate what you did."

"*De nada*, Red. Only do something for me now, okay?" he said. "Get that problem-solving sister of yours to help us find Trouble's owner. You can't keep passing him around like a soccer ball."

I will, Rockett decided as Ruben, Jessie, and Sharla took off. *I'll think about it seriously.*

For Trouble's sake, she knew she ought to set aside her funky feelings and try to call Juno.

There was a pay phone outside Mrs. Herrera's office. Rockett started down the hall toward it.

She's probably home by now, she thought.

And then she stopped and just stood there, in the middle of the hall, with kids rushing by in both directions.

Yeah, lounging in my room, her cool college wardrobe jamming my closet, her computer case hanging off my one decent desk chair, her laptop crushing my fabric swatches. Sure, I'll call her — and get the permanent busy signal that's the sure sign Juno's back in town.

Maybe she's not on the phone. Maybe she's at the kitchen

table, amusing Mom and Dad with her witty tales of college triumph. They totally forget I'm alive when she's around.

"Snap out of it, Rockett!"

Right. Snap out of it. Think about that little lost dog and his sorrowful owner — maybe a kid my age, maybe a little boy like my brother — who's probably worried sick, scouring the woods for him.

"What planet are you on? I've been trying to get your attention."

She looked up to find Nicole standing in the doorway of an empty classroom. The grieving girl was a mess, staring out at her, all splotchy-faced and impatient.

"Oh. I didn't hear you," she said.

"I couldn't exactly page you over the hall speakers. I need to see you." Nicole beckoned her into the room. "I mean, I need to see *someone*. And here you are. Have you been, like, wracked by my dilemma?"

"Well, I've given it a little thought," Rockett said. "You want to know what I think?"

"Not really. What I want is to be able to take charge of my buds again. To be the pushy prez they love, not some lame duck leader chafing under term limits."

Suddenly, Nicole threw her arms around Rockett, hugging her dramatically. "I can't believe my parents are doing this to me," she sobbed.

I can't believe my parents are doing this to me? Where have I heard that before? Duh, it's only what I've been whining about all day. Does that mean I'm thinking like Nicole now? Am I as stubborn and selfish as she is? Ugh, I wish she'd get off me. Enough with this weird bonding. I've got my own problems to solve.

"You think I should turn to my soon-to-be-ex-buds. But I'm already feeling so abused, so *discounted*," Nicole went on. "And I'm not talking about, like, your cut-rate, bargain-store discount. I mean discounted, as in dissed and counted out."

"There are things more important than your feelings," Rockett heard herself say, breaking out of Nicole's head-lock. "What other people want and need matters, too."

Other people . . . and puppies.

"You're not the only one suffering, Nicole. Do you have any idea how worried Steph and Whitney are about you?"

And what a mess Trouble is in because of me.

"Don't you think your true blues have a right to know what's going on?"

And don't my true blues deserve the most and best help they can get? The kind Juno has to offer?

"You don't know anything about human nature," Nicole wailed. "Friends can be so fickle."

"I disagree," Rockett said. "I think yours would stand by you. I think they'd do whatever they could to help you. And I think if you don't tell them what's really going on, you're gonna feel worse and worse. My sister once told me that stuffing your secrets can make you sick."

"I guess she's right."

"Yeah," Rockett said uncomfortably. "She's right about a lot of things."

100

For the first time all day that thought didn't totally irritate her. What did, however, was the realization that she had been thinking like Nicole. She *had* been stubborn and selfish, letting her own jealousy and pride keep her from asking Juno for help — help that Jessie and Trouble desperately needed.

"There you are!" Stephanie peeked in the door.

Whitney was with her. "Nic, we've been looking all over for you."

"Where'd you go after English?" Stephanie demanded. "We were waiting for you outside Tinydahl's room."

Nicole pulled herself together. "Rockett, don't you have something urgent to do? Someplace to go? Something to hide? A precious pet, perhaps? One whose future still rests in my capable, moisturized hands."

"Actually, I do have something important to do." Rockett slung her backpack over her shoulder. "I've got to make a phone call."

The hallway was still bustling with kids changing classes. Mr. Rarebit's room was at one end of the corridor. The pay phones were at the other. Rockett was torn about which way to go first.

It would be better, she decided, if she got a hall pass from art and then made the call.

She turned and ran smack into her favorite teacher.

"Ah, Rockett." Mr. Rarebit laughed, tossing back his gleaming black shoulder-length hair. "I'm flattered you're so eager to get to my class."

Rockett felt herself redden. "Art's my absolute favorite," she confessed, "but I was actually going to ask you if I could be a little late today."

"Tell me more."

"Well, it's kind of complicated, Mr. Rarebit, but I've got to reach my sister as soon as possible."

"A family emergency?"

She didn't want to lie.

"Sort of," she said. "My sister's just home from college for a couple of days and I need to try to reach her —"

"If anyone asks," Mr. Rarebit said, "tell them I gave you permission. They can check with me. But don't be too late. Class won't be the same without you."

"Thanks, Mr. Rarebit," she called, dashing toward the phones.

Miracle or coincidence, she wondered, when her home number rang through. Of course, no busy signal might just mean that Juno hadn't gotten there yet.

Her mother answered on the third ring.

"Hi," Rockett said. "I'm at school and I'm fine. Nothing's wrong. I just wanted to speak to Juno. Is she home yet?"

"Right here, Rock." Her sister had picked up the upstairs phone. "You can hang up, Mom," Juno said. "I'm on." Then she said to Rockett, "Hey, you miss me?"

Not even, Rockett wanted to grumble. But, to her surprise, she realized that she was smiling. Just hearing her sister's cheerful, teasing voice had made her grin.

That's the trouble with Juno, she thought. *You can't even be mad at her.*

"I've got a favor to ask," she plunged right in. "My friend Jessie found this adorable little dog out in the woods who I named Trouble, and we want to go on the Net to find his owner but, like, Arnold, who's this total cyber-geek, isn't sure what to do. Our message isn't even written yet although my bud Miko who's a way buff writer said she'd help out but we need it to be designed so that it's majorly outstanding and will definitely pull a response."

"Whew," Juno said. "So what's the favor?"

"Can you do it?"

"Do what?"

"If I get you a Polaroid of the puppy, can you write and design a site that will help us find a home for Trouble really, really fast. I can't even explain what's been going on but, Juno, believe me, we need to get him back to his owner right away."

"What do you mean fast? How soon?"

"Um, actually? Today would be good. But we can wait until tomorrow because Sharla's taking him home tonight."

Juno's laughter pealed through the phone. "So are you cleaning your room just for me? Are you completely thrilled that we're bunking together? Did you miss me so much you just couldn't wait for me to get home?"

"Are you going to help us?" Rockett tried to ignore Juno's teasing.

"Sure, I haven't got anything scheduled till tomorrow," Juno said, and then she started to cough.

"You will? Really?" Rockett asked.

"Yes, yes, yes." She was coughing again. "Bring me the Polaroid tonight," she wheezed. "I'll get everything else in motion. I gotta go," she said, clearing her throat. "I'll see you later."

"Juno," Rockett said, "how come you came home in the middle of the term?"

It was too late. Her sister had already hung up.

She waited for a moment, staring at the receiver in her hand, then she replaced it on the hook and went, "Yesssss!"

Mrs. Herrera was coming down the hall, heading for her office, with a ton of folders under her arm. "Aren't you supposed to be in class?" The principal cocked her head at Rockett.

"I'm on my way," Rockett explained. "Mr. Rarebit excused me to make this phone call. Family emergency," she mumbled.

"Judging by your enthusiasm, I'd say everything turned out all right. I hope mine do as well." She patted the folders she was carrying. "I've got a couple of family emergencies to deal with myself. Well, you'd better get going. You wouldn't want to miss art."

"It's my favorite subject," Rockett assured her.

"Mrs. Herrera!" A tall blond woman with a shiny brown leather briefcase in one hand and a cell phone to her ear, raced down the hall toward them.

"Mrs. Whittaker." The principal shifted her folders and held out her hand.

"Call me Celeste. Am I late?" the woman said, flipping shut her cellular and shaking Mrs. Herrera's hand. "I'm always late. But then my friends always forgive me. 'Celeste,' they say, 'you're worth the wait.' If only the judges I deal with were as bright. I have to remind them constantly, 'Hello, it's not me you're judging, your honor, it's my client.'"

It's Nicole's mother, Rockett realized. She's here to break the news to Mrs. Herrera that they're moving. Or maybe Mrs. H already knows. Maybe Nicole's leaving school is one of the family emergencies Mrs. Herrera is dealing with today.

"Rockett, move. Get going, girl." Mrs. Herrera shooed her. "I thought you loved art."

"I do, totally," she said. She hadn't even realized she was staring. It was just that Mrs. Whittaker sounded just like Nicole. Who, Rockett realized suddenly, would really be gone soon.

Duh. Like wasn't that what Nicole had been saying all along? Yeah, but it didn't seem real until just now.

She'd spent all her time trying to comfort Nicole, Rockett realized, walking slowly toward Mr. Rarebit's room, and none trying to understand why the girl was hurting in the first place.

As she passed the girls' room, Whitney came out blowing her nose. Her face was red, her eyes wet. In her hand was a hall pass signed by Mr. Rarebit.

"You knew," she accused Rockett miserably. "You knew Nicole's parents were planning to move and you never even told me."

"I couldn't, Whitney. She made me promise. I feel really

rotten about it, too — not just about not telling you, but also thinking about Nicole not being around. I mean, I haven't known the girl forever like you and Stephanie have, but she's as much a part of school as the Pine and Mr. Pill's meat loaf."

"I know," Whitney wailed. "What are we going to do?"

The excitement she'd felt after calling Juno had started to fade. A funny, hollow sadness began to take its place.

Whistling Pines Junior High without Nicole? It didn't seem possible.

On the other hand, Rockett mused, pushing down the icky feeling, *it might not be that bad*.

Whitney could run for class president. Maybe they'd become really good friends. And cheerleading would go on. Stephanie could take over there. In fact, with Nicole gone, more kids could participate in more stuff. And everyone would get a chance to make decisions, instead of just going along with one powerful person's opinion.

"It's too late to do anything," Rockett reported as they walked together toward the art room. "I just saw her mom talking to Mrs. Herrera. I guess they're working out the transfer right now."

"Nic wants to meet us at her locker after class. She told me to tell you." Whitney blew her nose again. "So how'd Ruben make out with the puppy?"

"Trouble ate his essay and wet the baby carrier."

"Get out. For real?" Whitney cracked a smile.

"Seriously. But my sister's going to help us. I just spoke

to her. She's going to design a monster Web message and get it on-line for us."

"Cool. Who's got the puppy now?"

"Sharla."

"Yeeew!" Whitney went. "No way."

"Way," Rockett confirmed. "She's excellent with him. And she's taking him home after school. Now all I have to do is borrow Mr. Rarebit's camera and get a Polaroid of Trouble to bring home to my sister. Then Juno's got all night to work."

"Is your sister a vampire? Doesn't she sleep?"

"Actually, I don't think so," Rockett said. "Tonight's gonna be a major nonwow for her. She's up all the time anyhow — cramming for exams, writing papers, doing extra-credit reading, plus she tutors and waitresses. And she's pulling a four-point-oh so far. Don't worry about Juno. She's practically bionic."

And it is so unlike her to take even a couple of days off from classes, Rockett realized. *Wonder why Juno decided to split in the middle of the semester? Wow, I can't believe I spewed all my needs at her before I even thought about asking what she was doing home.*

CHAPTER TWELVE

"The reason I called you all together," Nicole announced when Rockett, Stephanie, and Whitney were assembled at her locker, "is to offer each of you, who share my harsh secret, a souvenir — something to lessen your grief and remember me by."

Stephanie was crying. "Can I have a tissue?" she asked.

"Sure," Nicole said, swinging open her locker door. "Help yourself. I was thinking maybe you'd want my Whistling Pines cheerleading pom-poms, but if a tissue does it for you, be my guest."

"I think the tissue's just to wipe her eyes," Whitney explained.

"Well, yeah," Stephanie said. "And I was thinking more like your charm bracelet for the souvenir."

"Get over it," Nicole advised. "You want jewelry? You can have that lanyard you gave me in fourth grade. I think I still have it."

"But I made it for you," Stephanie pointed out.

"Hello, did you say 'no backsies'? I don't think so. Here," Nicole said after searching the pockets of a sweater she'd found on the floor of her locker. "You can have my mood ring."

"But it's so two years ago."

"Hello, that's what a souvenir's supposed to do, Stephanie — make you remember."

"I can't believe this is happening," Whitney said. "Nic, what are we going to do without you?"

"I know. Just thinking about it makes me want to cry, too," Nicole assured her, " 'cause you guys will be so lost without me."

The Polaroid that Rockett had taken of Trouble was in her backpack. She was eager to get home and give it to Juno. But she couldn't desert Nicole now. "Even if you're far away," she pointed out, "I mean, you know, with e-mail and everything, we can always stay in touch."

"Yeah, if there's electricity. The places Reggie was checking out were heinously remote. I'm talking more underdeveloped than Arnold Zitbomb. Which reminds me, Whitney — here, I want you to have this." Nicole took a jar of thick, slimy water out of the back of her locker.

"Yeeew," Whitney screeched. "What is it?"

"The science fair project Arnold did for me. It took honorable mention. It has something to do with plankton. It wasn't this ripe last year, but it's still a prizewinner."

"I don't want it." Whitney backed away and burst into tears. "I don't want a souvenir, Nicole. I want you. I want you to stay here at Whistling Pines, where you belong."

"Yes," Stephanie agreed, blowing her nose. "There must be something we can do. Maybe we could talk to your parents. Maybe they'd leave you behind. Let you stay."

"You could stay at my house," Whitney declared. "Ooooh, it would be so choice. We've got this cozy little guest room behind Daddy's den —"

Nicole blinked at her buds. "You care. You really care," she said in a strange voice, a voice that sounded, Rockett thought, as if Nicole were an awestruck little girl. As if it were her third birthday and she'd just gotten the shiny new bicycle she'd always wanted. Or some gleaming chauffeured limousine.

"You guys," Nicole crooned in practically a whisper, "you are so the best. How could I have doubted you?"

Then she quickly cleared her throat.

"Are we talking cozy as in professionally decorated with lots of floral fabrics and pastel pillows and deep pile wall-to-wall carpeting," she asked Whitney, "or are we talking cozy as in teeny-weeny, no TV, no walk-in closet?"

"You could share my TV," Whitney said.

"Take the jar," Nicole insisted. "You never know when you'll need a science project."

Through the noisy, end-of-day chaos in the hallway, Rockett heard a cell phone beeping. She turned toward the sound and saw Mrs. Whittaker taking a call.

"Look, Nicole," she said, "it's your mom. Stephanie's right. Maybe if you just told her how much this school means to you and we explained to her how important you are to Whistling Pines —"

"It's probably too late." Whitney's voice was thick with gloom. "She's already spoken to Mrs. Herrera. I bet your records and transfer papers are inside that briefcase. I bet she's coming to tell you to clean out your locker and say your good-byes, because it's *hasta la vista*, Nicole. You're booked on the no-frills flight to Bummersville."

"Stop, stop. It's too painful to think about," Stephanie said. "No electricity, no running water, no malls."

"Give it a rest, you guys," Nicole said, her chin beginning to tremble. "You're more depressing than Sharla's poetry."

"Nicole Anne!" Mrs. Whittaker called, flipping shut her phone. "I thought maybe I'd catch you before soccer practice."

"I don't have soccer today, Celeste," Nicole said icily.

"Cheerleading?"

Nicole glared at her mother.

"Piano lesson? Tae bo? Spin class? Whatever. I just came from Mrs. O'Hara's office —"

"Wow," Nicole said sarcastically. "No? Really? Duh, I wonder why. Could it be to discuss a crucial issue that you — oh, whoops, your bad — forgot to even mention to me?"

"Uh, it's Mrs. Herrera," Rockett told Nicole's mom softly.

"O'Hara, Herrera, whatever." Mrs. Whittaker brushed off the error. "Well, yes, we did discuss a potential crisis of sorts. But why would I mention it to you? I mean, I certainly would have if I thought you'd be interested.

111

I'll say this for the woman, she's on the ball. She under-stood the situation immediately and she's prepared to act on it."

"Oh, no. Oh, no," Stephanie sobbed.

"Say it isn't so, Mrs. Whittaker," Whitney begged.

"And where's Reggie?" Nicole demanded. "Out shop-ping for new luggage or buying an Esperanto dictionary?"

"A what?" Whitney asked.

"And who was flipping through a fashion 'zine in so-cial studies and, like, missed the section on Esperanto?" Nicole sharply inquired. "Let me guess, could it have been Barbara Whitney Weiss?"

"It's this international language someone invented, like, a hundred years ago," Rockett reported.

"Why would you think Daddy's out buying luggage?" Mrs. Whittaker asked.

"Duh," Nicole said. "You tell me."

"Well, I wish I could." Nicole's mother suddenly caught sight of the jar in Whitney's hands. "What is that? What are you girls doing?"

"Saying good-bye!" Stephanie blubbered. "Oh, Mrs. Whittaker. Please don't move!"

Staring nervously at the jar, Nicole's mother stood very, very still.

"That's not what she meant," Nicole grumbled.

"Please, please, we want Nic to stay here," Whitney explained. "To stay with us. Please don't make her go."

"If you girls have something planned, of course Nic can stay. Just don't be too late. I thought we'd have dinner at the country club tonight, as soon as Daddy's free. He's been on that computer for hours. Poor Reginald. He's researching investment properties in underdeveloped countries for one of his biggest clients. He's been at it all week."

"Investment properties?" Whitney said.

"For a client?" Stephanie mused.

"Reginald, my father? *That* Reginald? You mean he's not looking for a new home for us?"

"Well, if he finds the right investment for Alfred Farthington-Eps, perhaps he will. Although I'm very fond of our little place. And I did just have the tennis courts redone."

"Excuse me," Rockett ventured. "How come you were visiting Mrs. Herrera?"

"Well, I'm an attorney. And your principal had some legal questions about a fund-raiser the school is planning. Now, don't be too late, Nicole Anne." Mrs. Whittaker waved, whipped open her cell phone, and left them.

"Omigosh, omigosh, omigosh!" Whitney hugged the slime jar and jumped up and down ecstatically. "Nic. You're not leaving Whistling Pines. Your family's not moving. It was all a gigundo mistake!"

Nicole held out her hand to Stephanie. "My ring, please."

"But Nic, you just gave it to me."

"And you just said it was so sixth-grade. Anyway, I thought you wanted my charm bracelet. And I want you to have it," Nicole said softly.

113

"You can have the jar back," Whitney offered.

Rockett couldn't help it. She burst out laughing.

And then so did Stephanie and Whitney.

And finally Nicole laughed, too. "I am so back!" she hollered.

Stephanie cheered, "You're here to stay. How bangin' is that?"

"It's hot to death, girlfriends," Whitney agreed, high-fiving Rockett while Stephanie hugged Nicole. "Ones forever!"

"So cool," Rockett assured her. "Listen, you guys, I've got to get home and see how my sister's doing."

"Rockett's sister is going to help find out where the puppy belongs," Whitney explained.

"Well, everyone deserves a decent place to live," Nicole declared. "And thanks, Rockett. You know, for, like, being there."

"No problem. See you," Rockett called, hurrying to the main exit. She pushed open the school doors.

"Yo, Movado!" Sharla caught up with her. "What was that all about? I caught the tail end of that love fest back there."

Rockett laughed. "Where's Trouble?" she asked.

"Ruben and Jessie are keeping an eye on him. I just wanted to talk to you for a minute. I've been thinking," Sharla said as they stepped out into the sunlight and started down the steps. "You know, there are these people who get dogs for their kids and when the kids don't take care of them or the puppy turns out to be too much trouble, they, like, dump 'em. I'm thinking that's what might have happened to the little guy. Like maybe there's no one out there hunting for him. Maybe he got dumped by some jerk who didn't feel like taking care of him anymore."

"That's possible," Rockett agreed.

"Believe me, I know about these things."

"Really? You know a dog that got dumped?"

"Know one? I am one." Sharla laughed. "My old man dumped me and my moms. Like big wow, right? Forget him. But what I've been thinking is, whoever had the little mutt, well, they don't deserve him back, is what I think. I don't care if we never find the lamebrain who let him loose. Someone who can't take care of a puppy shouldn't have one."

"But what would we do with him?" Rockett asked. "I mean, would you consider keeping him?"

"What, like, for good? Put on your nightie, girlfriend, you must be dreaming," Sharla said.

She could be right, Rockett thought on the way home. Maybe Trouble didn't just wander away from his owner. What if someone had purposely left him in the woods, abandoned him? Whatever had really happened, they had to find him a home and fast. A good, loving home. The thought of the puppy pining away in a shelter was way too harsh.

Juno's car, the secondhand wheels their folks had gotten her just before she'd left for college, was in the driveway. Rockett saw the university parking permit on the windshield and noticed that her sister had left a pile of schoolbooks in the backseat.

Leave it to Juno to bring work home. Ms. 4.0 never takes a break.

She ran into the house and straight upstairs to her own room. Well, she thought, when she saw the door open and Juno's stuff all over her bed, it had been her own room yesterday.

Juno was at the computer, her back to the door.

"Hi," Rockett called. Pulling the photo of Trouble out of her backpack, she tossed the bag onto the guest bed, which looked as if it had already been slept in.

"Hey, short stuff. That you?" Juno called without turning around. Her voice sounded husky, like she was about to cough again. But she didn't. She cleared her throat and said, "I think I found your guy."

"No way!" Rockett hollered. She could hear the keyboard clacking like mad under her sister's swift fingers. Juno was on-line.

"Yup. Pure luck. Before I started, I checked a local message board. And I found this Lost Puppy message. The guy who posted it says he lives up near Hollow Brook Lake. Where'd you say Jessie found the dog?"

"There! Right up at the lake. Yesterday afternoon!"

Juno spun around on the desk chair to face Rockett. "I think he's the one. Jeffrey Westman's his name."

Rockett stared at her sister. Juno looked pale, almost pasty. And she'd lost a ton of weight. "Juno, are you okay?" she asked.

116

"Oh, no, don't you start on me, too. Mom and Dad have been driving me crazy. So how big is the puppy? This Jeffrey guy says his was really small, around four or five pounds tops; curly-haired, brown, mixed breed — probably part cocker spaniel."

"That's him. That's Trouble!" Rockett handed Juno the Polaroid. "I can't believe you found his owner so fast."

"I'll scan in the picture and see if he's the one. What a sweetie," Juno said, grinning at the photo. "He sure fits Westman's description."

"Did he say what happened?" Rockett asked.

"No, but he sounds like a good guy — genuine, concerned, cute."

"Cute?! How do you know he's cute?"

Hello, was that her never-flustered, fully-in-control sister blushing?

Radical yes!

"I mean," Juno fast-talked, "he seems to have a good sense of humor. He's serious about finding his dog, but not about himself."

Rockett raised an eyebrow. "Don't tell me you're crushin' on the boy?"

"Right, Rock. Like I really have time for romance."

"Maybe you should make time."

"Do me a favor," her sister said, so not subtly. "I'd love a cup of coffee. Think you could rustle one up for me? Black, no sugar."

"Sure," Rockett said. She couldn't wait to call Jessie

and Sharla, she thought as she hurried downstairs to the kitchen. The minute Juno was off-line and the phone was free, she'd blast the buff news. It had to be that guy. What was his name? Jeffrey something? West, Westlake? Something grown-up and serious-sounding. Westman. Jeffrey Westman, attorney at law. Dr. Jeffrey Westman. Professor Westman. A pipe-smoking, corduroy-jacket-wearing, walk-in-the-woods Juno kind of guy.

Juno had found him in, what, two seconds flat? She couldn't have been home all that long, either. She'd probably just walked in when Rockett called her from school. Her car was in the driveway. Duh. Obviously she'd driven down from college. Which was like a major trip. Had she gotten up at dawn?

She looked like it, Rockett thought. She had never seen Juno looking so tired.

Maybe that was why she wanted the coffee. And why the bed was all messed up. Maybe her sister had zoned when she got home, grabbed a quick nap, snoozed out. Which was so not a Juno thing to do.

Rockett was searching the kitchen cabinets, hunting for coffee, when her mom walked in and asked what she was looking for.

"Coffee, and nice to see you, too, Mom," she said, surprised at her own sarcasm. "I'm gonna fix a cup for Juno."

"Just what she needs, caffeine. No, you're not." Her mother sounded irritable.

And she was carrying a big pair of scissors!

Bright-colored paper and twisted wire jutted from the pockets of her work apron. Clearly she'd been in the middle of an art project, creating a new collage.

Maybe it wasn't going well, Rockett thought, because instead of being all happy that Juno was home, her mom seemed kind of edgy.

"Well, she asked me to," Rockett said.

"And I'm asking you not to." Her mother shook her head and sighed. She looked almost as beat as Juno, Rockett thought. Was there some mother-daughter virus going around?

"Come here," her mom said. "Come here. I'm sorry I'm so cranky today." She put down the scissors and opened her arms and, out of habit, Rockett walked into them.

It felt okay, she had to admit, to be standing there getting hugged by her mom. It felt like it had been a long time, too, since her mom or her dad had just reached out and hugged her.

What's going on here? she wondered. She was about to ask, too, when her mother released her and said, "Tell Juno to holler the minute she's off the computer, okay?"

"What should I tell her about the coffee?"

"There's decaf in the freezer. I'll fix some. Tell her I'll bring her a cup soon."

Rockett went back upstairs. "Mom's making the coffee," she said. Juno waved her hand in acknowledgment. She was still at the computer.

Rockett sat down on the bed. "So, did you scan in the picture?" she asked.

119

"The difficult we do right away, the impossible takes a little longer," Juno cracked. "It'll be another couple of minutes before I can send it."

"Are you on-line?"

"Not this minute."

Good, Rockett thought, *I'll call Jessie, then.* But she didn't move toward the phone. She just sat there staring at the back of her sister's head. "So how's it going? College, I mean," she heard herself say.

"I love it, but there's so much to do. So much reading, so many projects all due at once. What about you? How's life at Whistling Pines?"

"S'okay," Rockett said. "There are all these different groups there, and I'm not sure which one I belong to yet, but there are a lot of different kids I like. And my art teacher's really cool." She shrugged, though her sister wasn't looking at her. "I mean, it's not college and I'm not getting A's in everything."

Juno turned around. "Excuse me?" she said in her new, raw voice.

"Well, I just mean, I'm not you, Juno. I'd never have been able to find Trouble's owner in, like, half a day or anything."

"Being not me is a good thing to be right now," Juno said mysteriously. "Just ask Mom."

"Mom!" Rockett remembered. "She wanted me to let her know the minute you were off-line. I guess she's got a phone call to make or something."

"I guess," Juno said.

"And then I'm going to call Jessie and tell her that you found the guy who lost Trouble. She'll be so psyched. Juno, I hate to admit it, but you really are the bomb."

Rockett started to get up. "Wait," Juno said, pushing away from the computer. "What do you mean you hate to admit it?"

"Well, um, er, nothing," Rockett stammered, horrified at what she'd blurted out.

"Rock, are you steamed at me or something?"

"No way," Rockett said too quickly. "I mean, why would I be? You're doing this amazing solid for me and my friends. Just like I knew you would. I always know you'll back me. You back everyone. You're, like, this outstandingly supportive person. Plus you're practically a genius. Compared to you, my IQ's, like, room temperature."

She expected her sister to laugh at that, or at least crack a smile. But Juno didn't. She actually looked sad. She just sat there on Rockett's desk chair shaking her head as if she'd just heard the worst news ever.

"Juno!" their mother called. "Dr. Hawkins's office closes at four-thirty today. Are you off-line yet? Is the phone free?"

"I don't want to yell," Juno said to Rockett. "Tell her she can make her call now, okay?"

"What test results?" Rockett asked.

"I'll tell you in a minute. Just let Mom know, okay?"

121

Rockett did. Then she came back into the room. "She says she made decaf. It's downstairs if you want it. Are you sick?" she asked.

"They think I am," Juno said. "I've got this dumb little cough and they're acting like I'm dying."

"Is that why you came home?"

"Mom wanted me to see Hawkins. She says he's the only doctor she trusts. So I drove straight to his office and he ran these tests on me."

"I thought you looked kind of drained," Rockett said seriously. "Kind of pale, you know. Is it because of the blood tests?"

"The truth?" Juno said, clearing her throat again. "I'm wiped out, Rock. There's a lot more work this semester. And it's, like, always been important to me to make good grades. Mom thinks I'm doing too much extra stuff — waitressing, tutoring, and being, like, this unofficial teaching assistant to my design prof, and I'm also helping out a friend who works the front desk at our dorm. And I want to keep up my running, too. I need the exercise. I don't know. I'm just tired, I think."

Rockett didn't know what to say.

"Mom's afraid I may have mono. It's this virus that lowers your immunity, a bug that totally sidelines you."

"Mono?"

"Mononucleosis. Up at school they call it 'the kissing disease' because it can spread that way. Ha," Juno said, her voice all raspy and hoarse. "No chance I'd catch it, right?"

I've never seen Juno looking or sounding so down, Rockett thought.

As if her sister had read her mind, she said, "That was a joke, Rock."

Rockett wasn't so sure.

With this phony mega-watt smile, Juno insisted, "I'm okay. I'm going to be fine." Then she stood up and stretched. "And so is that little puppy. I bet your friends'll be glad to know he's got a home and someone who really seems to love him. It was Jeff Westman who put the all-points bulletin on that first message board I hit . . . and just about every other one I checked out. He, like, totally plastered the Net with lost puppy messages."

"Glad? Oh, they're gonna freak for sure," Rockett said.

She was right.

"No way," Sharla growled when Rockett reached her with the news. "No way am I turning this little doggie over to some bubbleheaded bozo who let him wander off into the woods by himself."

CHAPTER THIRTEEN

Juno drove Rockett to school the next morning. Rockett thought they'd be the first ones there, but just about everyone was waiting on the steps outside the main entrance.

They'd all showed up early: Jessie and Ruben, Arnold and Mavis, Max and Cleve, the CSGs, and The Ones.

Everyone was there but Sharla, Rockett noticed.

Jessie waved to her as she raced up the walk.

"Where is she?" Rockett asked breathlessly.

"Sharla?" Jessie looked around. "I don't know. She was here a second ago."

"She went around back to get a drink of water," Whitney said.

"Who cares if she's here, anyway? Where's Trouble?" Dana whined.

"Sharla won't tell anyone where she's got him stashed," Nakili told Rockett.

Miko said, "She wants to meet his owner first."

"Says she's got something to say to him," Cleve clarified.

"And it is going to be so totally, embarrassingly rude," Mavis prophesized.

"Is that her?" Nicole demanded as Juno climbed out

124

of the driver's seat. "Is that the lax Waldo, the clueless cadet, who, like, *misplaced* her pet?"

"That's my sister," said Rockett. "The owner's a man. Juno found him."

"So what'd she do, lose him again?" The rowdy cackle was unmistakably Sharla's. "Where is this supposedly brokenhearted bonehead?" she challenged, walking around the side of the school building with an empty pet carrier in one hand and Trouble cradled in her arms. The sleepy puppy looked fully content and comfortable. "Didn't show, huh? Too yellow? Or did he get himself lost? That's something he's really good at."

"There's my bootiful bow-wow," Dana squealed, rushing at the dog.

"Back off," Sharla snarled. "Nobody touches him. I only brought him out because he was getting lonely. He can't hardly stand to be anyplace but in my arms. And I have to admit, I'm getting kind of attached to the little mutt."

"Looks like it's mutual," Juno said.

"It does, doesn't it?" Sharla grinned at her. "Okay, so I promised I'd bring him and I did. I kept my part of the bargain. But I'm not turning him over to just anybody. So when's the skank who lost him showing up?"

"He said he'd be here by eight," Juno said. "It's only seven forty-five."

"What's the guy's name?" Max asked.

"Jeffrey Westman," Juno told him. "He seems really nice. He was so pleased that you guys had found the puppy and taken such good care of him."

125

"Nice? Don't make me gag," Sharla said. "You mean the guy's a dull doofus. I mean, even that name. Jeffrey Westman. Give me a break. That's a random Moe name if there ever was one. This puppy's a terrific little troublemaker. Loves mischief. He'd be miserable living with some boring guy with a name like Jeffrey Westman."

A motorcycle roared to a stop in front of the school. The rider, in jeans and a leather jacket, hopped off the Harley and hurried toward them. "Am I late?" he asked, unbuckling his helmet.

At the sound of his voice, Trouble began to wriggle and yip in Sharla's arms.

"Are you . . . *him*?" she managed to say.

He was twenty-something, Rockett guessed. He had curly brown hair, almost the same color as Trouble's. And green eyes that lit up at the sight of the little dog. And a huge, grateful smile, which he now focused on Sharla.

"I'm Jeffrey Westman," he said. "And you're Sharla, right? Sharla Rae Norvell?"

"He knows my name," she murmured. Trouble leaped suddenly, springing out of her grasp.

Jeffrey caught the puppy, who scrambled up his chest and began frantically licking his chin.

"Rockett told me all about you last night," he told Sharla. "It was cool of you to take care of him. I know I was a jerk to set him down. He's so little. I live about a mile from the lake. I put him down, got distracted by a noise, turned around for a second, and he was gone."

"*Jerk*'s kinda harsh. I mean, it could happen to anyone," Sharla said generously.

"Which one of you is Rockett?" he asked.

Dana raised her hand. "I am, I am," she shouted. Nakili elbowed her, hard. "I mean" — Dana pointed at Rockett — "she is."

"And this is my sister, Juno," Rockett said. "She's the one who found your message."

Jeffrey and Juno locked eyes.

"Juno," he said softly. "I wondered what you'd look like."

"She's usually not that pale," Rockett assured him.

"You don't go to school here, do you?" he asked.

"No, I'm up at the university," Juno answered, grinning at him. "I'm just home for a few days."

"When are you going back?"

"I was thinking I'd hang through the weekend," she said.

"Excellent." The biker smiled in dazed pleasure.

That's not a smile, Rockett thought, grinning to herself, *it's more like a promise.*

"And where's Jessie, the girl who found my dog?" he asked, reluctantly looking away.

Jessie was standing between Miko and Nakili, staring openmouthed at Jeffrey.

"Here she is," Miko said.

Nakili gave Jessie an encouraging push forward. "She's the one who rescued him."

"That's what I heard. Thanks," Jeffrey said. "Actually, I want to thank all of you —"

"We're totally open to a reward," Ruben advised him.

"Pizza?" Jeffrey asked, pulling his wallet out of his back pocket.

"Excellent," Cleve agreed, accepting two twenties. "We're all pigging out on pies for lunch!"

"Not a minute too soon," Arnold pointed out. "It's stew day in the cafeteria."

"Yuck. Mystery meat!" Whitney shuddered.

Stephanie made a face. "I don't even want to think about what Pill puts in his stew."

"I'm guessing it's narwhal," Mavis declared.

Jeffrey laughed as the puppy licked his face. "How's my Fred?"

"Fred?" Sharla wrinkled her nose. "Is that what you named him?"

"He just looked like a Fred to me." The biker shrugged apologetically. "I guess Trouble's his true name. Man, I searched the woods for hours. I still can't believe he made it all the way to the lake."

"Oh, no. Oh, no. I left my art project home!" Sharla wailed suddenly. "I promised Mr. Rarebit I'd have it finished today."

"Tragic loss," Stephanie snickered.

"Freeze-dry the attitude, Steph." Nicole shot her a curdling glare. "You wouldn't know tragic loss if you found it floating in your swimming pool."

"Nicky," her bud whined, "she's talking about those heinously depressing drawings she did."

"She gave Trouble a home," Whitney pointed out, "when nobody else would do it."

"Bingo!" Nicole said. "And therefore, no matter how rank her writing, we do not diss the girl. Not today, when the memory of my own brush with dislocation still stings. I am calling a twenty-four-hour halt to bad-mouthing people who provide homes to all creatures, great and small."

"Where do you live?" Jeffrey asked Sharla. "How about I give you a lift home, we pick up that project, and I'll have you back here before the bell goes off?"

"On your Harley?" Sharla was flipped.

"Yeah, I've got an extra helmet. And I brought Fred's crate."

"Fred?" Sharla shook her head as they walked toward his bike. "That's a really wimpy name," she said. "No offense. Maybe Fast Freddy?" she suggested.

As they roared away, Rockett walked her sister back to her car. "I'm glad you don't have mono," she said.

"Me too. But Doc Hawkins said the tests were borderline. Mom wants me to ease up on extra activities, like, give it a rest."

"I think she's right. I think you ought to chill, Juno."

"Or change my name to Fast Freddy?" her sister teased.

"I'd rather you slowed down," Rockett said. She tried to make it sound like a joke. "You know, so that I'd stand a chance of catching up to you."

Juno stopped and faced her. "Rock, you're not jealous of me, are you?" she asked point-blank.

Rockett looked away. *Come on*, she wanted to say, as if Juno were mental to even think such a thing. Then she changed her mind. "Actually," she said, staring down at her sneakers, "I guess I am . . . kind of."

Juno's hand was under her chin a second later, lifting her head. "Get out. Really, Rock? You're jealous of me? That is so funny. I can't believe it," her sister crooned.

"Funny?" Rockett wasn't sure she liked that.

"What I mean," Juno said, "is that I've been jealous of you forever."

"No way!"

"Yes, little sister," Juno assured her. "When you were born I thought my life was over. I mean, up until that moment, I was Mom and Dad's whole world, their everything. I was the cutest, the best, the baby. Then you showed up. Speaking of the right name. Along came Rockett. And zoom! I was left in the dust."

"Not even," Rockett said, laughing. "You were jealous of me? I don't believe it."

"Don't let it go to your head," her sister teased. "You were much cuter back then."

"Ha. You wish!" Rockett said. "So what's the plan, you going to hang out at home this weekend?"

"Just following doctor's orders," Juno said, grinning. "I'll stick around and chill for a couple of days. If you don't mind me sharing your room."

Rockett thought it over. "I don't mind. If you don't hog the phone."

"Give me a break, Rock. Practically everyone I know is away at school. Who's gonna call me?"

"Duh, let me think?" Rockett said.

"Okay, okay." Juno reached out and ruffled her baby sister's stick-straight hair. "You're thinking Jeffrey Westman, right?"

"How perfect would that be?" Rockett giggled.

"Way," Juno confessed.

"That would so be the bomb!"

Rockett's World ™

GET READY!
GET SET!
READ ROCKETT!

$3.99 each

☐ BDT 0-439-04405-7 #1: Who Can You Trust?
☐ BDT 0-439-06312-4 #2: What Kind of Friend Are You?
☐ BDT 0-439-08209-9 #3: Are We There Yet?
☐ BDT 0-439-08210-2 #4: Can You Keep a Secret?

Available wherever you buy books, or use this order form.

Scholastic Inc., P.O. Box 7502, Jefferson City, MO 65102

Please send me the books I have checked above. I am enclosing $_____ (please add $2.00 to cover shipping and handling). Send check or money order–no cash or C.O.D.s please.

Name_____Birth date_____

Address_____

City_____State/Zip_____

Please allow four to six weeks for delivery. Offer good in U.S.A. only. Sorry, mail orders are not available to

RW699

Meet me at

Find out more about these
great CD-ROM titles!

Camp brings new friends and
experiences ... are you ready?

What do dreams mean?